Trying to fit in . . .

Anna's eyes were swollen and her cheeks were streaked with tears.

"It's just a grammar quiz," Amy said. "Don't worry about it, Anna. If you want, we could all study for the next test together."

"It wouldn't help," Anna muttered. "Nothing will."

"What do you mean?" Elizabeth asked.

Anna shrugged. "I can't follow any of my teachers. I'll be lip-reading just fine, but then they'll turn around to write on the board or something, and I'll completely lose track of what's going on."

"Maybe if you talked to them and explained you're having trouble," Amy suggested.

"I've tried. My parents called Mr. Clark, too. He reminded all the teachers to be careful when they're lecturing, but I guess it's hard to break old habits." She shook her head sadly. "It's not their fault, anyway. It's mine, for being stupid enough to think I could ever fit in at a regular school."

SWEET VALLEY TWINS titles, published by Bantam Books. Ask your bookseller for titles you have missed:

SWEET VALLEY TWINS

Won't Someone Help Anna?

Written by
Jamie Suzanne

Created by
FRANCINE PASCAL

BANTAM BOOKS
TORONTO • NEW YORK • LONDON • SYDNEY • AUCKLAND

WON'T SOMEONE HELP ANNA?
A BANTAM BOOK 0 553 40633 7

Originally published in U.S.A. by Bantam Skylark Books

First publication in Great Britain

PRINTING HISTORY
Bantam edition published 1993

Sweet Valley High and Sweet Valley Twins are registered
trademarks of Francine Pascal.

Conceived by Francine Pascal.

Produced by Daniel Weiss Associates, Inc., 33 West 17th Street,
New York, NY 10011

Bantam Books are published by Transworld Publishers Ltd.,
61–63 Uxbridge Road, Ealing, London W5 5SA,
in Australia by Transworld Publishers (Australia) Pty. Ltd.,
15–25 Helles Avenue, Moorebank, NSW 2170,
and in New Zealand by Transworld Publishers (N.Z.) Ltd.,
3 William Pickering Drive, Albany, Auckland.

Printed and bound in Great Britain by
Cox & Wyman Ltd., Reading, Berks.

Won't Someone Help Anna?

One

"*Some*body's in big trouble!" Jessica Wakefield exclaimed as she entered the principal's office at lunchtime. Even through the closed door of his private office, Jessica could hear Mr. Clark yelling.

"He's just talking to a new girl who's enrolling today," explained Mr. Clark's secretary, Mrs. Knight.

"The poor girl's not even in school yet, and he's already yelling at her?"

"It's nothing like that," Mrs. Knight said. "I think the reason he's talking so loudly is because the new girl is deaf. She reads lips, and Mr. Clark's just trying to speak as carefully as he can so she'll understand him."

Jessica raised her eyebrows in surprise.

"We're going to have a deaf person in our school?"

Mrs. Knight nodded. "Her name is Anna Reynolds. She seems very nice." Mrs. Knight gave Jessica a warning look. "And I'm sure you'll make her feel welcome."

"Sure I will," Jessica said, although she wondered how she was going to make someone who couldn't even hear feel welcome. What should she do, write her a note saying *Welcome to Sweet Valley Middle School*?

The sound of Mr. Clark's voice broke into her thoughts. "Well, at least she isn't in trouble," Jessica said, gazing sympathetically at the principal's door.

"Speaking of trouble," Mrs. Knight said sternly, "what, may I ask, brings *you* here today, young lady?"

"Don't worry, I'm not in trouble this time." Jessica reached into her book bag and pulled out a piece of stationery. "I have a note from my mom. I have a dentist appointment this afternoon." She handed the piece of paper to Mrs. Knight.

"Hey, Jessica," said a familiar voice behind her. Jessica turned around to see Elizabeth, her twin sister.

"Hello, Elizabeth," Mrs. Knight said cheerfully. "To what do we owe the pleasure of your visit today?"

Jessica rolled her eyes. People never assumed that Elizabeth was in trouble the way they did with Jessica. That was only one of the many differences between them.

Jessica and Elizabeth *looked* exactly alike, right down to the dimples in their left cheeks. They each had long, sun-streaked blond hair and blue-green eyes. But Elizabeth was much more down-to-earth and responsible than her twin. She always did her chores without being asked and did her homework as soon as she got home from school. She spent a lot of her free time working on *The Sweet Valley Sixers*, the sixth-grade newspaper that she and her friends had started.

The idea of writing for fun made Jessica yawn. Her idea of a good time was gossiping with the other members of the Unicorn Club, which was made up of the prettiest and most popular girls in school. They had meetings at least once a week where they talked about clothes, movies, makeup, soap operas, and boys.

"So what *are* you doing here, Elizabeth?" Jessica asked.

"I'm picking up the letters to the editor from the *Sixers* mailbox," Elizabeth explained as she tore open one of the letters. "What about you? Did you get another detention?"

"For your information, I didn't do anything wrong," Jessica said. "I'm dropping off Mom's note about my dentist appointment."

Elizabeth was already absorbed in the letter she was reading. "Um . . . detention appointment?" she asked, distractedly turning over the letter.

"No, *dentist* appointment," Jessica said in exasperation. "What are you, deaf?"

Suddenly Jessica realized that Mrs. Knight was glaring at her.

"That kind of remark," Mrs. Knight said, shaking her head, "would be a good example of how *not* to welcome the new girl."

"What was that about a new girl?" Elizabeth asked as the twins stepped out into the hallway.

Before Jessica could respond, someone called out Elizabeth's name. The twins turned to see Cammi Adams heading toward them. Cammi was a sixth-grader who worked with Elizabeth on the *Sixers* staff.

"Elizabeth," she said in her soft voice. "Sophia's getting ready to type up that story I wrote about Julie Porter winning the music competition, and I wanted to check with you first to see if you wanted to make any changes."

"Are you kidding?" Elizabeth asked. "That story was perfect, Cammi. Your stories are always great."

"Thanks, Elizabeth," Cammi said, blushing.

Jessica smiled to herself. Cammi was definite nerd material. Jessica couldn't understand why her sister was always so nice to nerds like Cammi —but then, Elizabeth was nice to *everybody*.

"Listen, we're still going to need a profile

piece for next week's *Sixers*," Elizabeth said. "Can you think of anybody interesting?"

"I can," Jessica volunteered.

"Forget it, Jess," Elizabeth said with a sigh. "I already told you—we're not doing a piece on Rick Hunter. To begin with, he's a seventh-grader, and there's nothing that unusual about him—"

"He has gorgeous eyes," Jessica replied. "Anyway, that's not who I was talking about this time. You know that new girl you were asking about? Well, she's deaf."

"Deaf?" Cammi repeated, her eyes clouding. "There's going to be a deaf girl at our school?"

Jessica nodded.

"That's amazing," Elizabeth said. "How will she be able to understand things?"

"I guess she reads lips," Jessica said. She pointed down the hall to the office door. "She's in there right now with Mr. Clark. I'm surprised you didn't hear him yelling at her."

"But if she's deaf, why is Mr. Clark yelling?" Elizabeth asked.

"People are always doing that," Cammi said under her breath.

"What do you mean?" Elizabeth asked.

"Oh, nothing," Cammi said quickly. "I mean, I don't really *know* that, but I bet that people think if they talk louder, it will make it easier for a deaf person to read lips." She shrugged. "I'm just guessing though."

"You know, Jess, this is actually a good suggestion. If she's willing, let's do a profile of her," Elizabeth said. "It'd be a nice way to introduce her to the school." She smiled at Cammi. "And I think you're just the person to write it, Cammi."

"Me?" Cammi demanded, looking startled. "Why me?"

"You're the best profile writer we have," Elizabeth said as she browsed through the rest of her mail.

"Oh," Cammi said softly. She took a step backward. "Well, I . . . I guess I'll go tell Sophia about the story." Without another word, she dashed off.

Jessica shook her head as she watched Cammi leave. "Don't you think there's something a little strange about her?"

"Cammi? She's just shy," Elizabeth said. "She's really sweet. And she's a great writer. I don't know what we'd do without her on the *Sixers* staff."

"Well, she could use a little help with her wardrobe," Jessica said.

"We can't all be Unicorns, Jessica," Elizabeth said.

Jessica glanced back toward the office door. "I wonder what the new girl looks like. I've never met a deaf person before."

"Well, I'm taking a wild guess here, but I bet she's just like you and me, only she can't hear."

Jessica sighed. There was no point in discussing certain things with Elizabeth. Besides, Jessica had more exciting things to think about—like getting her cavity filled.

"Jessica? How's your mouth?" Elizabeth asked that evening.

Jessica was lying on her bed, reading a magazine. "I'm in agony," she replied weakly. "The pain is ex—uh, ex—"

"Excruciating?" Elizabeth offered.

"Yeah," Jessica said. "Excruciating."

"That's funny," Elizabeth mused. "I guess the pain wasn't bad enough to keep you from wiping out half a gallon of fudge ripple."

"Sorry, Lizzie, but I really shouldn't talk much. It's too painful." Jessica pointed at her mouth and shrugged.

"You could have left me a few spoonfuls at least," Elizabeth grumbled.

"It's painful for me even to say this," Jessica said, "but there are some ice-cream sandwiches in the freezer."

"Really? I didn't see any."

"That's because I hid them behind a big box of broccoli." Jessica sighed dramatically and climbed off her bed. "Come on, I'll show you."

The twins headed downstairs and found Mr. and Mrs. Wakefield reading in the living room. "How's your mouth doing, honey?" Mrs. Wakefield asked Jessica.

Jessica pointed to her jaw and shook her head.

"She's in excruciating pain, Mom," Elizabeth volunteered, rolling her eyes.

"Hey, who pigged out on all the ice cream?" the twins' fourteen-year-old brother, Steven, demanded, stomping into the room.

"Your sister did, and I told her it was all right," Mrs. Wakefield said. "She's in pain."

"Pain so excruciating, she can barely talk," Elizabeth added. "All she can do is eat. And eat. And eat."

"Well, if it keeps the midget's mouth shut, it's worth it," Steven said. "In fact, maybe we could work out some kind of a deal with the dentist to have her jaw wired shut permanently."

"Watch it, Steven!" Jessica warned. Suddenly her hand flew to her mouth. "Oops," she whispered.

"Jess, you're cured," Elizabeth cried. "It's a miracle!"

"I knew it was too good to be true," Steven complained as he followed them into the kitchen. Steven's girlfriend, Cathy Connors, was sitting at the kitchen table.

"Hi, Cathy," Jessica said with a smile. She and Elizabeth had helped get Cathy and Steven together. The twins really liked Cathy, although they still weren't sure what she saw in their brother.

"Hi, guys," Cathy said, looking up from the sheet of paper she'd been writing on.

"Want an ice-cream sandwich?" Jessica asked as she reached into the freezer.

"Sure," Cathy said. "Thanks."

"Wait a minute," Steven said. "I just looked in that freezer a minute ago—"

"You're getting senile, Steven," Jessica said, tossing him an ice-cream sandwich.

"Face it," Elizabeth told her brother. "You *are* nearly fifteen."

"Hmm," Cathy said, smiling. "Maybe it's time for me to look for a younger man."

"Hey, I'm like a great work of art. The older I get, the more valuable I am."

"Excuse me while I barf," Jessica commented.

"What are you working on, Cathy?" Elizabeth asked as she joined Cathy at the table.

"A guest list," Cathy said. "You know that little cottage on the beach that my grandparents have? Steven and I helped them paint it last weekend, and in return they said we could have a beach party there." She laughed. "That is, as long as we promised to end it by eleven thirty and not invite the whole school."

"We're going to have a barbecue, and Cathy and I are going to make all the food," Steven said. "Spare ribs, potato salad . . . the whole bit."

"You two are so lucky," Jessica said. Suddenly she was filled with jealousy. High school was so much more exciting than middle school. It would be ages before she could have her own party on the beach. She could just imagine walking with Rick along the shore, holding hands—it would be so totally romantic.

"Hey, I've got a great idea," Cathy exclaimed. "Why don't you two come?"

"Us?" Jessica and Elizabeth exclaimed happily.

"*Them?*" Steven echoed in disbelief. "No way!"

"It's half my party, Steven," Cathy said firmly, "and I want them to come. They can even invite a few friends, if they want."

Jessica gasped. She couldn't wait to start calling the other Unicorns to give them the good news. "How many friends?" she asked Cathy.

"Zero," Steven replied. "Nada. Zilch."

"Just do me a favor and don't invite everyone in the sixth grade," Cathy said with a laugh.

"This is so nice of you, Cathy," Elizabeth said.

"This is so insane of her," Steven muttered.

"Come on, Steven. What can it hurt?" Cathy said, giving him a playful nudge.

Steven stared at the floor, pouting. Jessica watched him nervously. Suddenly she regretted all the nasty things she'd ever said to him. Still, if she apologized now, it would probably seem a little obvious.

"Well . . ." Steven said at last. He eyed the twins, tapping his fingers on the table. "I *suppose* I could let you come. Of course, with all those extra guests, there's going to be that much more cooking to do—not to mention cleanup."

"We'll help," Jessica cried eagerly. "I love to cook, don't I, Elizabeth? I got a C+ in cooking class last grading period—"

"Thanks for the warning," Steven said. "You can be in charge of cleanup."

"No problem," Jessica replied with a smile. She'd do anything to be able to go to a high-school party with real live high-school guys.

"Thanks, Cathy," Elizabeth said gratefully.

"And thank *you*, Steven," Jessica added, giving her brother a big hug.

Steven made a face and shrugged her off. "Just promise me one thing, OK?"

"Anything," Jessica vowed.

"Whatever you do, don't hug me at the party."

Two

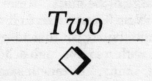

"First spelling word," said Mr. Bowman, the twins' English teacher. "Accommodate."

Jessica raised her hand. "Mr. Bowman? I couldn't study last night because I had to have a cavity filled yesterday, and I was in too much pain to—"

"Come on, Jessica," Mr. Bowman said. "Is that the best excuse you can come up with? Pretty lame, by your standards."

"But—"

"If you don't know the answer, fake it," Mr. Bowman advised.

Jessica frowned, her pencil poised over a blank sheet of paper. *Acomadate*, she wrote at last.

"Next word," Mr. Bowman said. "Excruciating."

"Finally," Jessica whispered. "A word I know!"

There was a knock at the door, and Mr. Clark stepped into the room. "Are we interrupting anything?" he asked.

"No, no," Mr. Bowman said. "Come right on in." He turned to the class. "Time out, folks. I know you'll all be heartbroken to hear we'll have to finish up the spelling quiz tomorrow."

Mr. Clark cleared his throat. "We've got a new student joining us today," he said. "Her name is Anna Reynolds."

"I like her already," Lila Fowler whispered to Jessica. Lila was a Unicorn and one of the richest girls in school. "Anybody who interrupts a quiz is okay by me."

"It's that girl I told you about," Jessica whispered back. "The one who's deaf."

"Class, meet Anna," Mr. Clark said. He held the door open, and Anna stepped in from the hallway.

Jessica stared at her in disbelief. *This* was the deaf girl? She didn't look at all the way Jessica had imagined she would. Anna was Asian, with long, straight black hair, almond-shaped eyes, and a brilliant white smile. She was stylishly dressed in white leggings and a pink hand-painted T-shirt that almost reached to her knees. If Jessica hadn't known better, she would have thought Anna looked like potential Unicorn material.

"Anna, we all want to welcome you to Sweet Valley Middle School," Mr. Bowman said. Jessica noticed that he was looking directly at Anna as he spoke, saying each word slowly and distinctly.

"Folks," Mr. Bowman continued, turning to face the class, "Anna is hearing-impaired, but she can lipread quite well. She's going to be attending classes here in the morning and three afternoons a week. Monday and Wednesday afternoons she'll be going to special classes with other hearing-impaired students."

"Amazing," Lila whispered to Jessica. "She doesn't *look* deaf."

Jessica scanned the room. Everyone seemed a little uncomfortable. Some people were staring at the floor or doodling on their desks.

Mr. Bowman turned toward Anna again. "Would you like to say a few words, Anna?"

Jessica frowned. Weren't deaf people usually mute? It hadn't occurred to her that Anna would be able to talk.

Anna stepped confidently to the center of the room. "Hi, everybody," she said with a bright smile. Her words were a little fuzzy, but Jessica could understand them easily. "I'm really sorry about interrupting your quiz," Anna continued. "I know how disappointed you all must be."

Everyone laughed, and the tension in the room seemed to dissolve.

"Well, Anna," Mr. Clark said, forming his words carefully. "I'll leave you in Mr. Bowman's capable hands. Let me know if you need anything."

"Why don't you take a seat in the third row, Anna," Mr. Bowman suggested. "There's an empty seat next to Cammi Adams."

Poor Anna, Jessica thought. *Stuck sitting in Nerdville, USA.* She turned around to watch Anna get settled. When Anna smiled at Cammi, Cammi seemed to shrink into her seat.

Cammi could at least try to be a little friendly, Jessica thought. *It wouldn't kill her. And it's practically her social duty, since Anna's sitting next to her.*

Jessica was glad she didn't have that responsibility. It wasn't that she wouldn't be friendly to Anna—but what could she possibly have in common with a girl who couldn't hear?

"Let's ask Anna to sit with us at lunch," Elizabeth suggested to her best friend, Amy Sutton, as they walked out of English class.

"Good idea," Amy said.

The two girls fell into step beside Anna. "You already seem to know your way around," Elizabeth remarked.

Anna paused in midstride, frowning. "Sorry," she said with an apologetic shrug. "I didn't catch that. I can only lipread if you're looking right at me."

"Oh, I'm sorry," Elizabeth said, feeling awkward. "I didn't know—"

"How could you?" Anna said. She gave Elizabeth a friendly smile. "You probably don't do a whole lot of lipreading in your everyday life."

"You're right about that," Elizabeth said, smiling back. "I'm Elizabeth Wakefield, and this is Amy Sutton. We were wondering if you'd like to sit with us in the lunchroom."

"Unless you're leaving to go to your other school," Amy added.

"I've got one class after lunch here, and then my mom picks me up," Anna replied. "And I'd love to eat with you. I'm starving!"

After Amy and Elizabeth retrieved their lunches from their lockers, the three girls headed to the cafeteria. Amy and Elizabeth joined Julie Porter and Maria Slater at their usual table, while Anna stood in line to buy her lunch.

"Anna really speaks well, doesn't she?" Elizabeth said as she unwrapped her sandwich.

"Except for a few words," Amy agreed. "Sometimes she's a little hard to understand, or she talks a little too loudly."

"Yeah," Julie said with a laugh. "Just like you when you've got your Walkman on."

"I wonder if she's ever been able to hear," Maria said.

"We could ask her," Amy suggested. "She doesn't seem to mind talking about being deaf."

"Here she comes," Elizabeth said. "You know, one of us really should have warned her about the cafeteria food."

"It's stuffed green peppers today," Amy said

with a laugh. "Believe me, one taste and she'll realize why we all bring our lunch."

"It does look pretty bad," Anna said as she sat down. "And by the way—no, I don't mind talking about being deaf."

Amy's eyes widened. "Wait a minute. You were all the way over in line when I said that. How could you tell what I said from that distance?"

"As long as I can see your mouth clearly, I can understand you." Anna grinned. "I guess there are some advantages to being deaf."

Anna plunked down a large salad, a cup of yogurt, and two apples.

"Great," Julie joked. "A health-food freak." She stared guiltily at her bag of potato chips.

Anna laughed. "I guess I should confess it right up front—I am kind of a health nut. I love exercise, especially aerobics." She paused long enough to give a big smile to Ricky Capaldo as he passed by. Ricky blushed and smiled back.

"You work fast," Elizabeth teased.

"Just wait!" Anna said with a laugh. "That's what I like best about this school so far—there are so many boys. And they're all so cute!"

"Where?" Julie asked. "Have I missed something?"

"Let's see," Anna said. "I've been here three hours so far, and here's my list. Aaron, Bruce, Jerry, Ken—"

"That's Ken Matthews," Elizabeth said. She pointed to Amy. "Amy and he are sort of—"

"OK," Anna said. "Cross Ken off the list. But that still leaves Peter, Ross, Todd—"

"Well, Elizabeth and Todd—" Amy began.

Anna laughed. "There's still Winston and Lloyd—"

"Lloyd *Benson*?" Amy asked doubtfully.

"Sure," Anna said. "He's cute, in kind of a klutzy way."

"Anna, I have got to introduce you to my twin sister," Elizabeth said as she reached over to steal one of Julie's potato chips. "You're both boy-crazy."

"Whoops," Anna said. "We just had another fadeaway. That's what I call it when I miss some words."

"Sorry," Elizabeth said. "I wasn't looking at you, was I?"

"No biggie," Anna said with a wave of her hand. "Happens all the time."

"It must be frustrating for you," Elizabeth said sympathetically.

"Well, I try to look on the bright side," Anna said. "At least I don't have to wear a hearing aid. And in a way, I don't really know what I'm missing. I lost my hearing when I was only eighteen months old, after I got this disease called meningitis."

"How did you learn to speak so well?" Julie asked.

"I've been going to special schools for as long as I can remember. That's where I learned lipreading, too."

"It must be hard," Amy said.

"It is," Anna said. "Usually it's impossible to understand every single word someone says." She paused. "A lot of words look just alike. Watch me when I say these: *Mat, bat, pat.*"

Elizabeth shook her head. "They look exactly the same."

Anna grinned. "Or how about this: *Put that dog on a leash. Put that dog on a leech.* See? *leech* and *leash* look exactly the same."

Everyone laughed. "So how do you figure things out?" Elizabeth asked.

"A lot of times you can tell from the context. And you watch faces and gestures. Some people are easier to read than others." Anna paused to pour dressing on her salad. "I'm still having trouble following some of the teachers. Fortunately, it gets easier the longer you know a person. But in the end, sometimes all you can do is guess and hope for the best."

"This is so interesting, Anna," Elizabeth said. "Listen, would you consider doing an interview for the sixth-grade newspaper? A bunch of us write for it, and you'd be perfect for a profile."

"Me?" Anna asked. "Just think of it." She clasped her hands over her heart and fluttered her lashes. "A celebrity!" She laughed, but then her face grew serious. "Actually, I think it would be a great idea. Sometimes it takes hearing people a while to figure out how to act around a deaf person. Maybe I could give them a few pointers and make people feel more relaxed about it. Mr. Clark told me this is the first time Sweet Valley Middle School has had a hearing-impaired student, so I really want everything to go okay."

"Who's going to do the story, Elizabeth?" Julie asked.

"I asked Cammi to do it," Elizabeth said. She twisted around in her chair to see if she could find Cammi. As usual, Cammi was sitting in a corner of the lunchroom, her head buried in a book. "I'd call Cammi over to introduce you, but it looks like she's in the middle of a good book," Elizabeth said.

"I know how that is," Anna said as she picked up one of her apples. "I love to read. It's one thing I can do where hearing isn't important."

"So, do you communicate with sign language?" Amy asked.

"Sure," Anna said. "We call it ASL, for American Sign Language. I wish more people knew it. It's really a pretty language. Sort of like hula dancing, you know? Where you tell a story with your hands." She put down the apple and moved her hands quickly in a variety of shapes.

"What was that?" Elizabeth asked.

"Your name," Anna replied. "I spelled it using the basic letters of the alphabet. But there are also hand gestures that communicate ideas. Some of them are really pretty easy to guess." She thought for a second. "Like this." She hunched over and pretended to scratch her side. "What word was that?"

"Well, you looked like a monkey," Julie said, giggling.

"Exactly," Anna said. "Here. Try another one." She cupped her hands, covering one with the other. The thumb of her bottom hand peeked out and bobbed up and down.

Elizabeth cocked her head to one side. "Well, it looks like a little animal, maybe. I know—how about a turtle?"

"Right!" Anna exclaimed. "Now, this one's a little harder." She put the knuckle of her index finger at the corner of her eye, as if she were wiping away a tear.

"That's easy," Julie said. "You're sad."

"Nope." Anna shook her head.

"There's something in your eye?" Amy ventured.

"I'll give you a hint," Anna said. "It stands for a piece of food. Remember—ASL is very poetic."

"I'll bet it's an onion," Elizabeth said.

"Not bad," Anna said, pushing her tray away. She pointed to Julie's food and raised her eyebrows hopefully.

"What did that mean?" Julie asked.

"Oh, that wasn't ASL," Anna said with a

laugh. "I was just wondering if I could have one of your potato chips!"

Just stop thinking about it, Cammi told herself as she trudged home that afternoon. But she couldn't get the picture out of her mind—the picture of Anna Reynolds sitting in the lunchroom with Amy and Elizabeth and Julie, laughing and talking as if they were old friends. As if there were nothing at all different about Anna.

"It won't last," Cammi muttered under her breath. Sooner or later the novelty of having a deaf friend would wear off. Then people would show their true feelings.

Cammi turned the corner and crossed the lawn toward her house. Her dog, Ludwig, a big, shaggy brown mutt, wagged his tail and stood up on stiff legs. Ludwig was older than Cammi. He was a wedding present to her parents, and despite the fact that he was a little homely, they loved him almost like another child. Ludwig was much more than just a pet—he was an important part of the family. He had many more responsibilities than most dogs.

"Hey, Lud," Cammi said, reaching down to stroke his head. Despite his arthritis, he always insisted on greeting Cammi when she got home. "I hope your day was better than mine."

Ludwig wagged his tail and waddled behind Cammi into the house. Cammi's seven-year-old sister, Cara, was sprawled out on the couch, watching TV.

"Hi, Cara," Cammi said as she flopped down next to her. "What're you watching?"

"One of those talk shows. This one's about people with secret lives. See that gross-looking guy on the end?" Cara pointed toward the screen. "He's got *five* wives!" She wrinkled her nose, which was covered with freckles. "I can't believe one lady would marry him, let alone five."

Cammi laughed in spite of her bad mood. As she stared at the TV screen, a string of words slowly streamed across the bottom, small white letters on a black background.

"By the way," Cara said, "Dad got home from work early. He's in the kitchen with Mom."

Cammi nodded, her eyes still glued to the people on the show. People with secret lives, Cara had said. People with something they were trying to hide. "I know how they feel," she said, more to herself than to Cara.

"Why?" Cara asked hopefully. "Do you have a secret? Come on, Cammi, tell me. I promise, cross my heart, I won't tell anybody, except maybe Shawna." Shawna was Cara's best friend. "And she won't tell."

"Shawna already knows my secret," Cammi muttered. "And so do you, for that matter."

"I *do*?" Cara frowned. Cammi could tell that Cara was trying to remember all of her big sister's past sins. "Oh, you mean about the time you ate that whole cherry pie and then blamed Ludwig?"

"No, Cara," Cammi said, sighing. "I mean—" she glanced at the kitchen, "Mom and Dad."

Cara's eyes clouded. "But that's not a secret. All my friends know."

"Well, all *my* friends don't."

"I don't get what the big deal is," Cara said.

"You've just been lucky so far. Kids can be . . . they sometimes aren't very nice."

"My friends are nice. Or else they wouldn't be my friends."

Cammi stood. "I know, but sometimes kids just don't understand things. They're—well, they're mean to people who are different. People like Mom and Dad."

"I know some mean kids, too," Cara replied, tilting her head.

"What do you say to them when they're mean?" Cammi asked, half hoping for a good answer.

Cara shrugged. "I call them booger-heads."

"Great, Cara," Cammi said, rolling her eyes. "I'll definitely keep that in mind. You want anything to eat from the kitchen?"

"I already had two peanut butter and banana sandwiches."

Cammi headed for the kitchen, with Ludwig slowly following at her heels. She paused in the kitchen doorway. Her parents were sitting at the table, their backs to her. They were talking to each other, their hands moving swiftly, as if they were conducting an orchestra together.

They had no idea she was there. She might as well have been invisible.

Just then, the telephone rang. Instantly the light over the kitchen table began to flash. Ludwig's ears pricked up, and he trotted over to Mrs. Adams and nudged her hand.

As she stood to get the phone, Mrs. Adams noticed Cammi and smiled. She touched her husband's shoulder, and he, too, turned around and smiled.

"I'm home," Cammi said, her hands moving skillfully. She didn't bother using her voice.

Her parents had never heard it.

Three

◇

"What does a capital *T* stand for?" Jessica asked. It was Wednesday evening, and Jessica was helping Steven and Cathy make cookies for the party. She stared at a recipe in Mrs. Wakefield's cookbook.

"Big T?" asked Steven, who was sitting at the kitchen table. "That's a teaspoon."

"Try again, Steven," Cathy said as she pulled a bag of flour out of the pantry. "It's a *table-spoon*."

"Wrong, Betty Crocker," Steven said firmly. "It's a teaspoon."

"How would you know, Steven?" Jessica demanded. "The only thing I've ever seen you make is cold cereal."

"Hey, I'm quite the gourmet chef," Steven

said, propping his feet up on the table. "And I'm absolutely, positively, sure that it's a teaspoon."

"Where's Elizabeth?" Cathy asked. "Let's let her settle this."

"She's watching TV in the family room," Jessica answered. "She said something about too many cooks spoiling the cookies. But she promised to clean up when we were done."

Steven leaned back in his chair, his fingers laced behind his head. "Trust me, ladies. It's a teaspoon."

"Tablespoon," Cathy said.

Steven rolled his eyes. "Teaspoon."

"Tablespoon."

"Teaspoon."

"Tablespoon."

Steven grinned. "Tablespoon."

"Teaspoon," Cathy said automatically.

"Aha!" Steven cried. "What did I tell you, Jessica? Cathy agrees with me."

"No fair," Cathy cried. "You tricked me."

Jessica laughed. "Would you two please stop arguing? I'll look it up in the back of Mom's cookbook."

"We're not arguing, Jessica," Cathy explained, leaning over to give Steven a quick kiss. "We're just having a very loud conversation."

Jessica looked up from her cookbook and smiled. Those two really did make a cute couple —even if Steven *was* half of it.

"So, what's the verdict?" Steven prompted.

Jessica scanned a page at the back of the cookbook. "Found it!" she cried. She shook a measuring spoon at her brother. "And it's a *table*-spoon, phlegm-brain."

"Hey, it's not too late for me to uninvite you to the beach party," Steven warned.

"Oh, yes it is," Cathy countered. "I need her to help me make these cookies, since you're proving absolutely useless."

"I'm supervising."

"Here," Cathy said, shoving a mixing bowl and a spoon into Steven's hands. "Supervise these."

Steven scowled. "How many kids have you invited, anyway, Jessica? Not the whole munchkin brigade, I hope."

"I just invited a few of my closest personal friends," Jessica said evasively, pretending to concentrate on her recipe.

"How *many* close personal friends?"

Jessica shrugged. "Well, I had to invite all the Unicorns, of course."

"Of course," Steven said sarcastically.

"And they had to invite a few guys," Jessica added. "I invited Rick Hunter, and Lila invited Jake Hamilton, and—well, you get the idea."

Steven sighed. "Why didn't you save time and just issue an invitation over the loudspeaker during morning announcements?"

Jessica raised her eyebrows. "Hey, now that you mention it, Steven, that's not a bad idea."

* * *

"How are the cookies coming?" Elizabeth asked.

Jessica dropped onto the couch with a groan. "We've only made the first three batches, and I'm already exhausted. Plus, the last batch was a little well-done."

"How bad?"

"Well, Steven put the fire out, if that's what you mean."

Mr. Wakefield came into the family room and sniffed the air. "Do I smell something burning?" he asked.

"That's Steven, Dad," Jessica explained. "He's practicing for the barbecue."

"He's not burning charcoal in the kitchen, is he?" Mr. Wakefield asked in alarm.

"No, he's *making* charcoal. Out of cookies."

Mr. Wakefield looked puzzled. "Just try not to burn down the house, OK?" He shook his head and walked away.

Jessica got up. "Well, Lizzie, back to the embers."

"Good luck." Elizabeth turned back to the program she was watching.

"Elizabeth?" Jessica said. "Why are you watching the TV without any sound?"

"I'm trying to read lips," Elizabeth explained. "The way Anna Reynolds does. You wouldn't believe how hard it is."

Jessica concentrated on the screen for a moment. "There!" she said. "That guy in the hat just said hello."

Elizabeth rolled her eyes. "No kidding, Jess. He was waving."

Jessica watched a little longer, but she soon grew frustrated. "They talk too fast," she complained. "And they keep turning their heads so you can't see their lips."

"See what I mean? It's really hard, isn't it? I don't know how Anna does it."

Jessica brushed a spot of flour off her jeans. "I'm kind of surprised they let a deaf girl into school, aren't you?"

"What do you mean?"

"Well, we were talking about it at the Unicorner today. And it just seems to us that Sweet Valley Middle School should be for, you know, *normal* people."

Elizabeth stared at Jessica, her eyes narrowed.

"Why are you looking at me that way?" Jessica cried. She flopped back on the couch and closed her eyes. "We didn't mean it *meanly*, Elizabeth."

"What way did you mean it?"

"We meant it in a *helpful* way." Jessica opened one eye and peeked at Elizabeth.

"That's the Unicorns, all right," Elizabeth said sarcastically. "Helpful, kind, considerate. Sort of like Girl Scouts, only better dressed."

"Very funny, Elizabeth. We were just worried about Anna not fitting in."

"Have you given her a chance?"

Jessica sighed. "Come on, Elizabeth, I don't have to make friends with every misfit in school." She smiled at her twin. "Everyone knows that's *your* job."

To Jessica's relief, Elizabeth laughed. "Look, Jessica," she said. "Anna's *not* a misfit. I've had lunch with her the last two days, and she's really cool and really nice. I wish you'd give her a chance. You two have a lot more in common than you realize."

"I doubt that."

"She's completely boy-crazy, for one thing. And she loves clothes. Today she told me she has this incredible T-shirt collection—"

"Really?" Jessica sat up. "She does wear cute shirts. How many does she have?"

"I don't know," Elizabeth said, shrugging. "A hundred or so, I think."

"Are you kidding? She has a hundred T-shirts?"

"Something like that. I didn't pay much attention to that part of the conversation. We were talking about a lot of really interesting stuff."

"The T-shirts *are* the interesting stuff."

Elizabeth smiled. "Well, I'm sure Anna would love to tell you all about them. I invited her to go to Casey's Place tomorrow after school. Want to come along?"

"What if I say no?"

Elizabeth thought for a moment. "I'll tell Steven how many people you've really invited to the barbecue."

"You may seem nice on the outside, Elizabeth Wakefield," Jessica said, "but deep down inside you're just as sneaky as I am, you know that?"

Elizabeth grinned. "Where do you think I learned all my tricks?"

"I don't see why we have to come," Lila complained the next afternoon.

Jessica paused at the entrance to Casey's Place. "Because I may need moral support. I've never talked to a deaf person before."

"Mary Wallace sits next to Anna in science," Ellen Riteman said. "She said she's really nice."

"Mary's just like Elizabeth," Jessica said dismissively. "Always looking on the bright side."

Lila nodded. "I hate it when people do that."

"How did Elizabeth talk you into this, anyway?" Ellen asked.

Jessica opened the door to Casey's and stepped inside. "Blackmail," she answered.

As usual, the ice cream parlor was packed with students. Jessica glanced around and spotted Elizabeth sitting with Anna and Amy at a table near the back.

"Jess! You made it!" Elizabeth said as Jessica and her friends approached. Jessica noticed that her sister was speaking distinctly and looking at Anna as she talked.

"Anna," Elizabeth said, "this is my twin sister, Jessica, and her friends Lila Fowler and Ellen Riteman."

"Hi," Anna said with a grin. "I've seen you all around school, but it's nice to actually meet you."

"Nice–to–meet–you," Jessica said, speaking in slow motion and moving her lips in an exaggerated way to make sure Anna understood what she was saying.

Anna laughed. "Just talk like you usually do," she urged. "I'll get most of it."

"Really?" Ellen asked.

Anna frowned. "Are you chewing gum?"

Ellen looked surprised, then nodded.

"That does complicate things, Ellen," Amy said, rolling her eyes.

Ellen spit out her gum and stuck it underneath the table.

"Very sophisticated," Lila muttered.

"Wow!" Anna said as Jessica, Lila, and Ellen sat down. "Three Unicorns at once. I'm really honored."

Jessica paused for a moment to see if Anna was kidding. After all, she *had* been spending time with Elizabeth and Amy. They might already have contaminated Anna's mind on the subject of the Unicorns.

"You mean, you know who we are?" Lila asked.

"Of course," Anna said. "*Everybody* knows who the Unicorns are. Let's see. Janet Howell's the president. She's in eighth grade, and she's your cousin, right, Lila?"

Lila nodded, looking surprised.

"You all love Johnny Buck and *Days of Turmoil*," Anna continued. "You try to wear something purple every day, and a bunch of you founded the Boosters, the middle-school cheering squad."

"Amazing," Jessica said. "You've only been in school three days, and you already know all that?"

"It's simple," Anna said with a shrug. "I just do a lot of eavesdropping!"

Everyone laughed, and Jessica found herself starting to relax. "Elizabeth told me you're really into aerobics," she said.

Just then a waitress approached the table. "Two hot-fudge sundaes," she said, placing huge bowls of ice cream in front of Elizabeth and Amy. "And one fruit salad with extra cottage cheese," she added, handing the plate to Anna.

"There must be some mistake," Jessica protested. "You didn't actually *order* that, did you, Anna?"

"Anna's not just into aerobics," Elizabeth said. "She's into health food, too."

Anna held up a spoonful of cottage cheese. "Anybody want a bite?"

Jessica made a face. "Aerobics I can understand. But eating curdled milk for fun? No way."

Anna looked down at her cottage cheese with a dubious expression. "Thanks for putting that image in my mind, Jessica," she said. "Now I'll *really* enjoy this stuff."

"So you don't actually like cottage cheese?" Jessica asked.

"Not very much," Anna confessed. "But I want to be an aerobics instructor when I grow up, so I'm trying to learn good eating habits now. Maybe by the time I'm an adult, I won't still love to pig out on ice cream. I mean, you can't be an aerobics instructor if you have monster thighs."

For a moment, no one said a word. *How can you be an aerobics instructor when you can't hear music?* Jessica wondered silently.

"Go ahead," Anna said to Jessica. "Ask."

Jessica shifted uncomfortably. It seemed like Anna could read minds, too. "Well," she said, "I was wondering how—" She paused, hoping she wasn't about to put her foot in her mouth.

"You were wondering how I can dance without hearing music, right?" Anna said, laughing.

"Well, yeah, now that you mention it," Jessica said.

"I can feel the beat of the music through the floor," Anna explained. "As a matter of fact, I'm a pretty good dancer, if I do say so myself. I've even been thinking about starting an aerobics club here at school. What do you think?"

"I guess that would be a good idea," Jessica said doubtfully. "I've always wanted to take an aerobics class."

"It'd be good for all the Boosters to take," Lila said. "*Some* of us could use the exercise." She cast Ellen a warning look as Ellen swiped a spoonful of Elizabeth's ice cream.

"Don't look at me," Ellen said defensively. "I get plenty of exercise."

"Such as?" Lila prompted.

"Ellen does a lot of finger aerobics when she pushes the buttons on her TV remote control," Jessica said.

Anna laughed. "Well, that's three people who are interested, anyway. How about you, Elizabeth?"

"Sure. It sounds like fun."

"I thought I'd post some sign-up sheets around school," Anna said.

"How much would it cost?" Jessica asked.

"It'd be free," Anna said. "It's just so I can get some practice and stay in shape."

"Well, then it's a really great idea," Jessica said. It was hard not to get caught up in Anna's enthusiasm. "I'll give you a hand with the sign-up sheets if you want."

"Great! I can't wait to get started," Anna said excitedly. She gave Jessica a sidelong look. "After the first class, you can tell me whether you think I can keep up with the music."

Suddenly Jessica had an idea. "Anna," she said, "my brother and his girlfriend are having a beach party on Saturday. There'll be plenty of dancing, and since you're into that, I was wondering if—"

"Thanks, Jessica," Anna said, "but Elizabeth already invited me. I'm really excited, too. I hope you invited plenty of eligible guys!"

"You bet!" Jessica smiled. It was amazing. Ten minutes ago, she had been dreading this meeting. But now she had to admit that for once in her life, her twin had been right about someone. Anna really *was* nice. Maybe Elizabeth wasn't such a bad judge of character after all.

Four

◇

Cammi slipped into the girls' bathroom and held her breath. She knew she couldn't keep avoiding Elizabeth forever, but she was hoping that if she gave it enough time, Elizabeth might forget about the Anna Reynolds article.

Cammi stared into the mirror and thought of Cara. "You're being a booger-head, Cammi Adams," she whispered with a grim smile. But she couldn't help herself. She didn't want to write about a deaf person. She already knew all she needed to know about deaf people.

Her own brown eyes stared back at her. *Admit it*, she told herself. *The real reason you don't want to write this article is because you're afraid that somehow the truth about your own parents will come out.*

"Cammi?"

Cammi spun around to find Elizabeth peeking in the door. "I thought I saw you head in here," Elizabeth said.

"Was that the warning bell I just heard?" Cammi asked. "I really should get going. I was late to Mr. Nydick's class last week, and he practically had a fit."

"I'll walk with you," Elizabeth said.

Cammi nodded and followed her out into the crowded hallway. She might as well get this over with. There was no way she could avoid Elizabeth forever.

"Before I forget," Elizabeth said, "my brother, Steven, and his girlfriend are having a barbecue tomorrow. They're letting Jessica and me invite a few friends, and I thought maybe you'd like to come."

For a moment, Cammi felt a little surge of excitement. She'd already heard about the big party. Caroline Pearce, the biggest gossip in the sixth grade, had told her all about it. But it had never dawned on Cammi that Elizabeth would actually invite her.

"Everyone on the *Sixers* staff is coming," Elizabeth added.

Cammi sighed. It figured. Elizabeth probably felt that she *had* to invite Cammi, the one real loser on the staff.

"I'd like to come," Cammi began slowly.

"But I have to baby-sit my little sister, Cara. You know how it is."

Actually, it wasn't Cara that Cammi had to worry about. It was her parents. They were having workmen come over to fix the driveway, and they wanted Cammi to be there to help communicate with them. That kind of thing happened all the time. Because their speech wasn't very clear, Mr. and Mrs. Adams often asked Cammi to help them with everyday things, like talking to bank tellers or phoning friends. In some ways, Cammi felt more like an adult than a kid.

"The party should last till eleven," Elizabeth said as the girls turned the corner. "Maybe you could come later."

"Maybe, but I doubt it." Cammi pointed to the drinking fountain. "I need to get a drink of water," she said, hoping Elizabeth would go on without her. But Elizabeth just followed her over to the fountain and waited patiently.

"Have you had a chance to interview Anna yet for the *Sixers* profile?" Elizabeth asked when Cammi had finished drinking.

Cammi shook her head. "I've been awfully busy," she said. "I've got that big social studies paper due, and it seems like I've had tons of homework all week."

"That's OK," Elizabeth said as they continued down the hall. "No rush. I think you'll really have a good time writing it though. I'm sure you and Anna will really hit it off."

"Why do you say that?" Cammi asked suspiciously. "It's not like we have anything in common."

"That's just what Jessica said, and she and Ellen and Lila really had a good time with Anna at Casey's yesterday."

Cammi wanted to laugh. She knew the Unicorns would be the first ones to get tired of Anna, though she couldn't exactly say that to Elizabeth.

She paused at the next corner. "Well, I have to get going, Elizabeth," she said. "I promise I'll get around to that interview as soon as I can."

"Trust me. Anna's really great," Elizabeth said. "And after a while you practically forget that she's hearing-impaired."

Cammi watched Elizabeth walk away. "You never *really* forget, though," she muttered under her breath. She turned toward Mr. Nydick's door. As she did, she caught a glimpse of Anna out of the corner of her eye. She was talking to Jessica and some of the other Unicorns, smiling and laughing as if they were all the best of friends.

It won't last, Cammi told herself. The novelty of having a deaf friend would wear off soon enough, and the Unicorns would forget Anna even existed.

Anna would find that out, sooner or later. She wasn't what people thought of as "normal." She never would be. And in this world, Cammi knew that what mattered most of all was being just like everyone else.

* * *

"Rise and shine," Elizabeth called on Saturday morning. She tapped lightly on Steven's door.

"Try again," Jessica suggested. "Harder."

This time Elizabeth really pounded. "Steven," she called. "It's practically noon."

"Open up, Steven!" Jessica yelled. "We made you breakfast, and your stupid cereal's getting soggy."

Elizabeth waited another minute, then cracked open Steven's door. Steven lay motionless on his bed with a pillow over his head.

"Bummer," Elizabeth said.

"What?" Jessica asked, following her sister in.

Elizabeth poked at one of Steven's feet. "He's dead."

"Does this mean the party's off?"

"We could have it anyway," Elizabeth suggested. "Sort of like a wake."

Jessica set down the breakfast tray they'd prepared next to a pile of dirty socks on Steven's floor. "Phew," she said. "What *is* that smell?"

"Could be the socks," Elizabeth ventured. "Or it could be the dead body."

"All right, all right," Steven moaned, tossing aside his pillow. "I'll get up. Just leave me in peace!"

Jessica picked up the cereal bowl and waved

it over Steven's face. "We made your favorite, Steven. *Space Critters.*"

Steven cracked open one eye. "Why are you munchkins being so nice to me?"

"Hurry," Elizabeth urged. "The little green marshmallow aliens are starting to drown."

Slowly Steven sat up while Elizabeth plumped a pillow and placed it behind his back. "What did you do? Wreck my bike? Steal one of my shirts and ruin it? Break my CD player?"

"As a matter of fact, we've already packed your CD player in the car so Dad can drive it over to the party," Elizabeth said. "We got up extra early so everything would be ready. You and Cathy won't have to do a thing." She pulled a piece of paper out of her jeans pocket with a flourish. "Listen to this. CD player and CDs?"

"Check," Jessica said.

"Volleyball and net, Frisbees, softball bat, and catcher's mitt?"

"Check," Jessica said.

"Plates, napkins, and silverware?"

"Check."

"Food, soft drinks, and ice?"

"Check."

"Earplugs?"

"Earplugs?" Steven echoed.

"For Cathy's grandparents," Elizabeth explained. "In case things get too noisy."

"You *did* think of everything," Steven said. He shook his head in amazement. "Tell you what.

You two can come to all my parties if you'll always do this much work."

"Deal," Jessica said enthusiastically.

"By the way," Steven said. "Next time I'd like scrambled eggs if it's not too much trouble."

"Come on, Jess, let's get out of here," Elizabeth said with a groan. "I liked him better when he was dead."

By three o'clock that afternoon, the beach party was in full swing. To Jessica it seemed as though half of Sweet Valley Middle School had shown up, but Steven and Cathy were having such a good time that they didn't seem to notice.

In fact, everybody seemed to be having a good time. Some kids were lying in the sun, swimming, or playing volleyball. Others were hanging out near the big stone barbecue pit, where all the food was set out. And a group of dancers was gathered closer to the cottage, where Steven had positioned his speakers.

"Great party," Jessica said to Cathy's grandmother, who was sitting on the porch in a lounge chair.

"I'm sorry, dear. What did you say?"

"I said it's a great party," Jessica yelled over the blare of the speakers.

"I'm sorry, dear, but I don't know any Marty."

Jessica considered trying one more time, but instead she decided to smile and move on. "Nice talking to you," she said with a wave. She grabbed Cathy as she passed by. "I think your grandma's using the earplugs we brought, Cathy."

"I wish you'd brought some for the neighbors," Cathy joked. "Although, so far, no one's complained." She ducked just in time to avoid a close-flying Frisbee.

"Sorry," Jake Hamilton yelled.

"You nearly decapitated me!" Cathy yelled back with a laugh. She turned to Jessica. "Who is that guy, anyway?"

"Jake Hamilton," Jessica answered. "He's in seventh grade."

"He's got a cute smile." She winked at Jessica. "Maybe you should go play some Frisbee."

"He's Lila's," Jessica explained. "Well, sort of. They went to a dance together. Besides," she added, nodding toward the spot where a bunch of guys were playing volleyball, "I kind of like Rick Hunter."

"That's right," Cathy said, raising her brows. "I forgot you two were married for a while."

"Just for two weeks, during that marriage project for health class," Jessica said. "Besides, most of the time Rick just teases me and drives me crazy. You know what his nickname is for me?"

Cathy shook her head.

"Airhead!"

Cathy laughed. "That just means he likes you."

"Well, I thought he did. But he hasn't even said hi to me yet today." Jessica pouted.

"Maybe you should make the first move."

"What do you mean?"

"You know, maybe ask him to dance. Show him you're interested." She nodded toward the cottage. "I'd better go refill the ice bucket. Good luck with Rick."

"Thanks, Cathy," Jessica said. She watched Cathy run over to Steven. They kissed each other, and Jessica couldn't help smiling. She really did like Cathy. Having her around was almost like having an older sister. *Steven's awfully lucky*, she thought. *A guy with socks as smelly as his really doesn't deserve such a great girlfriend.*

Jessica sat down near the barbecue pit and watched Rick from a distance. She was smoothing sunscreen on her legs when she heard Elizabeth call her name.

Jessica turned to see Elizabeth and Todd Wilkins walking across the sand toward her. "Isn't this party turning out great?" Elizabeth asked.

Jessica gazed toward Rick. He looked up and smiled.

"So far, so good," Jessica said.

"Did you see Anna out there?" Elizabeth pointed toward the area where people were dancing. "I'll bet she's danced with every guy here. But she seems to be spending most of her time with Jim Sturbridge."

Jessica laughed. "She doesn't waste any time."

"Speaking of dancing," Todd said, gesturing toward the dancers. "Want to?"

"I thought you'd never ask," Elizabeth exclaimed.

Jessica watched her sister and Todd join the other dancers. It looked like so much fun, she could hardly keep herself from moving to the beat.

"Hey, Jessica."

Jessica turned to see Rick standing behind her. "Rick!" she exclaimed. "Hi."

There was a long, awkward pause that seemed to go on for a hundred years. What had Cathy advised? *Ask him to dance. OK*, Jessica thought. *Why not?*

"Hey, Rick, I was wondering if you, um, want to, um, you know—" Jessica said, pointing toward the dancers.

"Dance?" Rick asked with a laugh. "You're actually asking me to *dance*?"

Great advice, Cathy, Jessica thought silently. *He obviously thinks I'm some kind of mega-dweeb.*

"Don't do me any favors, Hunter," Jessica said hotly. "I'm sorry you think it's so hilarious."

"No, no," Rick said, grabbing her arm. "I was laughing because I was just about to ask *you* to dance."

"Really?"

"Would I lie to you, airhead?"

"Probably, bonehead," Jessica replied. "What about your volleyball game?"

"It's OK," Rick said, leading her toward the dancers. "We were losing, anyway."

As she and Rick started dancing, Jessica looked across the sand and noticed Anna moving gracefully in perfect rhythm. Jessica wondered if she could feel the beat through the sand. *Probably not*, she thought. *Maybe she's just moving in the same tempo as everyone else.* However she did it, she looked like she was having a great time.

Jessica smiled and waved. "Having fun?" she called.

Anna nodded, grinning broadly. "I think I'm in love!" she mouthed silently. "I wish it would never end."

Jessica didn't need to be a lipreader to know how Anna felt.

Five

◆

"It's your turn," Cara signed to Cammi late Saturday afternoon.

Cammi glanced at the Monopoly board and sighed. Usually she loved playing board games with her family, but today she just couldn't seem to stay interested.

"Are you okay, honey?" Mrs. Adams asked in sign language.

"Fine," Cammi signed back. Although her parents could manage some normal speech, the whole family used sign language at home. Even Cammi and Cara spoke sign language to each other when their parents were in the room, since reading lips was difficult for Mr. and Mrs. Adams.

"She's just mad because I put a hotel on

Boardwalk," Mr. Adams teased, smiling as he signed.

For what seemed like the hundredth time that day, Cammi glanced at the telephone. She'd started to dial Anna's number so many times that she had it memorized.

"You can stare at the phone all day, but it's not going to make anyone call," Cara joked, her fingers moving swiftly. Suddenly, as if on cue, the living room lights began to blink. "Wow," Cara said out loud. "I guess you *can* make people call."

Cammi sighed and got up to answer the phone, even though she knew that the call probably wasn't for her. Beside the phone was a device called a TDD, which stood for Telecommunications Device for the Deaf. When the TDD was connected to the phone, it enabled Mr. and Mrs. Adams to send and receive written messages, which appeared in green letters on a small electronic screen.

Mr. and Mrs. Adams had several deaf friends who owned a TDD. One deaf couple, the Humphries, had a daughter named Lynne who was Cara's age. Although both girls could hear, they liked to send each other messages on the TDD. Cara called Lynne her "telephone pen pal."

"Who is it, Cammi?" Mrs. Adams signed.

Cammi glanced at the TDD screen. *Hi, Cara!* she read. *How R U? It's me, Lynne. GA. GA* meant *go ahead.* People used abbreviations on the TDD so they could fit more words on the screen.

"It's just Lynne," Cammi signed to her mother.

Mr. Adams rolled his eyes, giving Cara a patient smile. "How am I ever going to win this game if it keeps being interrupted?" he signed.

While Cara sent a message back to Lynne, Cammi rolled the dice and moved her piece around the board. She landed on Chance and picked up one of the orange cards. *Go Directly to Jail*, it read.

"Too bad," Mrs. Adams signed, giving Cammi a sympathetic smile. "You're having rotten luck today, honey."

Cammi shrugged and moved her piece to the jail square. She thought about how sometimes living in this house felt like being trapped in jail. No one came in, and she couldn't ever escape.

Even as a small child, Cammi had realized that her house wasn't like any of the others on the block. Sometimes it seemed to be full of invisible gremlins that made strange things happen to all of the household gadgets. When she turned on the TV, words appeared at the bottom of the screen. When someone pushed the doorbell, lights began to blink in the house. When the smoke alarm went off, all the lights flashed crazily. Even Cammi's parents' alarm clock was different. When it was time to wake up, their bed began to vibrate.

"Come on, Cara," Cammi urged. "It's your turn."

Cara typed in one last message and then ran back to the game. "OK, I'm ready."

"What did Lynne say?" Cammi asked.

"She asked me to her birthday party," Cara responded. "I can't wait!"

Cammi looked away, remembering Elizabeth's invitation to the beach party. Maybe she should have gone. It was so easy for Cara to make friends—why was it so hard for her?

But she *couldn't* have gone even if she'd wanted to, she reminded herself. She had to be here all day to help her parents with the workmen. She had duties and responsibilities that other kids didn't have.

Of course, she had school responsibilities, too. And one of those responsibilities was writing for the *Sixers. You're going to have to call Anna sooner or later*, she told herself. *You might as well get it over with.*

"I have to make a call," she signed to her parents.

"It must be a boy, the way you've been hesitating," Mr. Adams teased.

Cammi forced a smile. "It's just this new girl I'm supposed to interview for the paper." Before she could change her mind again, Cammi went to the phone and dialed Anna's number. "Is Anna there?" she asked when Mrs. Reynolds answered.

"She's at the Wakefields' beach party," Mrs. Reynolds said. "May I take a message?"

I should have known, Cammi thought resentfully. Anna was friends with both the twins. Of course she'd be at the party.

"Would you ask her to call Cammi Adams?" Cammi said, giving Mrs. Reynolds her phone number. "But tell her there's no rush. No rush at all." She hung up the phone. *With any luck at all,* she thought, *Anna will forget to call back.*

"Not home?" Mrs. Adams signed.

"No," Cammi signed back. "She's at a party."

Both her parents looked at her with an expression of concern. "Weren't you invited?" her mother signed.

"Sure, I was invited."

"Why didn't you go?" Mrs. Adams pressed.

Cammi shrugged. "I had stuff to do," she responded. "Besides, you guys needed me."

Mrs. Adams glanced at her husband, then reached over to touch Cammi's arm. "Honey, you should have told us you had a party to go to," she signed.

"We don't ever want you giving up things because you think you need to help us," Mr. Adams signed. "I know it's hard to believe, but we got along pretty well for several years before you were even born."

"I don't mind helping you," Cammi signed quickly.

"We know that. But we want you to have fun, too," Mrs. Adams signed.

"I know, Mom," Cammi answered. Then she forced a bright smile. "Come on, let's play."

"You're just anxious to get out of jail," Mr. Adams signed good-naturedly.

Cammi didn't answer. It was true—she did want to get out of jail. More than her parents could ever know.

Early that evening, Rick's friends recaptured him for one last game of volleyball. Jessica had just decided to go for a walk along the beach when Lila caught up with her.

"Where are you going?" Lila asked as Jessica paused by the huge bonfire a bunch of high-school guys had built.

"I'm going somewhere where I can explode without hurting any innocent bystanders," Jessica replied.

"Explode?"

"Lila, I ate three hot dogs, tons of that potato salad Cathy made, and about a dozen toasted marshmallows. I need the exercise."

"Well, let me know if you see Jake," Lila said. "I haven't seen him in hours."

"Maybe he's playing volleyball with Rick."

"I'll go check," Lila said hopefully. "And try not to explode." She grinned. "You'd ruin that new T-shirt."

Jessica started off across the sand, veering toward the water's edge where the wet sand was easier to walk on. The sun glinted on the water as it slowly set in a blaze of red and gold.

After a few minutes Jessica noticed two people walking up ahead of her near a pile of huge rocks. She squinted. One of the people definitely looked like Jake. But she couldn't be sure who the other one was. For a minute she considered going back to get Lila. But the thought of running all the way back to the bonfire seemed like too much work.

Jessica trudged along, letting the sea foam rush over her toes and keeping her gaze on the sunset. Suddenly she stopped. She was under the shadow of the rocks. But she obviously was not alone.

Through a space between two of the huge boulders, she could just make out Jake talking to someone. The light was getting dimmer every second, but she was pretty sure the someone was a girl.

It's not like I'm spying or anything, Jessica told herself as she crept closer. *I have a right to walk along the beach. Even if I am walking very, very quietly.*

The girl turned slightly, and Jessica recognized her in a flash.

Cathy! What was Cathy doing in the rocks with Jake?

Jessica knew that there was no way she'd ever be able to see clearly—let alone hear clearly —from her position. Slowly she began circling around the largest of the rocks, hoping to find a better angle. For an agonizing few minutes Cathy and Jake were out of sight, but then Jessica found a crevice that let her creep up much closer than before. The crashing surf was still too loud for her to hear their conversation. But from her new position she could make out Cathy's back clearly, and beyond her, the shadowed figure of Jake.

Suddenly Jake put his arm around Cathy's waist and drew her close. It was dark, but not so dark that Jessica couldn't tell what was going on.

Cathy and Jake were kissing.

"Look, Elizabeth, just sit down, OK?" Jessica pleaded that evening. She pointed to Elizabeth's bed. "I don't want you to be standing up when I tell you this because you might faint and fall down and hit your head, like Storm Winters did on *Days of Turmoil*. She ended up with amnesia."

Elizabeth stared skeptically at her twin. "How exactly did you get to be so weird, Jessica?"

"I am not any weirder than usual," Jessica shot back distractedly.

"That's not all that reassuring."

"Lizzie! Just sit down, OK?"

"Oh, all right," Elizabeth said, settling down on the bed.

"Ready?"

"Ready."

"What is the most amazing thing I could possibly tell you?" Jessica whispered.

Elizabeth thought for a moment. "Hmmm. That you're going to quit the Unicorns?"

"Come on, this is serious." Jessica took a deep breath. "Let me put it this way. What's the worst thing I could possibly tell you?"

Elizabeth thought again. "That you want me to join the Unicorns?"

Jessica shook a warning finger at her sister. "You're going to feel really bad about joking around when I tell you what happened. I saw them with my very own eyes, so don't try and tell me I didn't because I—"

"Saw who? What are you talking about?" Elizabeth asked, looking perplexed.

"Cathy and Jake!" Jessica paused, waiting for her sister's gasp.

"Cathy and Jake?" Elizabeth repeated. "So what? I saw them at the party, too."

"Not like *I* saw them. They were *together*, Elizabeth."

Elizabeth looked at her sister suspiciously. "What are you talking about?"

"Cathy and Jake were kissing."

Elizabeth hesitated. "No way." She crossed her arms over her chest. "What do you mean, exactly?"

Jessica gave her twin a superior smile. "Oh, so now you're interested."

"Are you trying to tell me that Cathy—

Steven's Cathy—and Jake Hamilton—were actually kissing?"

Jessica nodded.

"Like a friendly peck on the cheek?"

"No. Like a *very* friendly kiss on the lips."

"Where did you see this going on?" Elizabeth asked, still sounding suspicious.

"Down by the rocks on the beach. During a very romantic sunset."

"So it was dark?"

"It wasn't dark. Not totally. Anyway, I know what I saw. I was only about ten feet away."

"I'm sorry, but I don't believe it," Elizabeth said, although she didn't sound completely confident. "Cathy would never do that. Besides, Jake's only in seventh grade."

"Yeah, but he's very cute."

"So's Steven," Elizabeth pointed out loyally.

"Oh, *please*, Elizabeth. We're talking about our brother here. You know, loud burps, stinky socks. And facts are facts. Cathy's tired of Steven. She's dumping him." Jessica sighed dramatically. "He's going to be totally crushed."

"I hope you're wrong, Jess."

"That's all you can say?" Jessica cried. "You *hope*? We need to *do* something. We can't just let Cathy do this to Steven behind his back. He may be a jerk sometimes, but he is our brother."

Elizabeth lay back on her bed. "And what exactly are you thinking of doing?"

"We have to tell him. That way he can dump

her before she dumps him. What if other people find out before he does? He'll be humiliated."

"Forget it, Jessica. This is none of our business. Steven and Cathy should handle their relationship by themselves."

"What relationship? She's making a fool out of him!"

"Jess, you are *not* going to tell Steven any of this. You shouldn't have been spying in the first place."

"I wasn't spying," Jessica said hotly. "I was just walking along, enjoying the sunset, and digesting hot dogs!"

"I'm serious. If you're wrong and you go blurting this to Steven, you could mess up their whole relationship."

"They don't *have* a relationship," Jessica argued.

"And even if you're right—and I don't think you are—how would you break this to Steven?" Elizabeth shook her head. "I sure couldn't bring myself to do it."

Jessica hesitated. Elizabeth had a point. It would be horrible. "All right," she said reluctantly. "I won't say anything. At least not for a while."

Just then the bedroom door opened, and Steven stuck his head in. "One of you munchkins left your beach bag downstairs, and Mom says it's leaking sand all over the carpet. Go clean it up before I get stuck doing it."

Jessica nodded her head meekly. "Thanks, Steven. I'll take care of it right away."

Steven narrowed his eyes. "The party's over. Why are you still being so nice?"

"You need *someone* to be nice to you," Jessica said, ignoring Elizabeth's scowl.

Steven shook his head. "Nice try, twerp. But I'm not picking up your stuff."

Steven closed the door, and Jessica flopped down on the bed next to Elizabeth. "He's so sweet," she said sadly. "He's going to be totally shattered."

Six

◇

On Sunday afternoon, Cammi rode her bike over to Anna's house. "Come on over," Anna had said cheerfully that morning when she'd returned Cammi's phone call. "I'll tell you everything you always wanted to know about being deaf, but were afraid to ask!"

I already know more than I ever wanted to, Cammi thought to herself as she rang Anna's doorbell.

A moment later, the door swung open, and Anna appeared. She was wearing a T-shirt with the hand configurations for the letters of her name printed across the front.

"It's my name," Anna said, noticing Cammi's gaze.

"I know," Cammi said without thinking.

"You know how to finger spell the alphabet?" Anna asked as she held open the door.

"No, I just—" Cammi hesitated. "I just figured that's what it had to be. Your name has four letters, and there are pictures of four hand positions."

Anna smiled. "Most people just stare at me blankly when I wear it."

"Doesn't that bother you?"

"It used to. But after a while, you just sort of shrug it off." She laughed. "Once, I was downtown with my parents, and we were all signing. This girl across the street was staring at us like we were from Neptune or something. She was so busy looking at us that she walked straight into a wall!"

Cammi laughed uneasily, thinking back on all the times she'd felt embarrassed with her own parents in public.

"That's the gang," Anna said as they passed a family room, where a football game was blaring on the TV. "My older brothers, Sean and Alex. This is Cammi Adams, guys."

Cammi waved shyly at the two boys, who smiled and waved back.

"You can leave them out of the article," Anna added under her breath.

"What article?" Sean asked, overhearing Anna's comment.

"I'm going to be famous," Anna said.

"Cammi's writing an article about me. And she just happens to be the best writer on the paper."

Cammi felt her cheeks burn. "Who told you that?" she asked.

"Elizabeth," Anna said matter-of-factly. "She says you're great."

"She'll have to be if she's going to make *you* look good," Alex teased. As he spoke, he also signed. That way, Cammi knew, he could be sure that Anna caught all his words.

"Just ignore him," Anna advised. "I may be hearing-impaired, but at least I'm not brain-impaired like he is." She walked over to the coffee table and grabbed the TV remote control. "Here," she said. "Let me show you something cool."

"Hey," Sean complained. "It's fourth down and three, and they're going for the TD!"

"This'll only take a second," Anna said, waving him off. She switched to the all-music video channel. "They close-caption lots of shows on TV," Anna explained. "See the words running across the bottom? They tell you what the people on the screen are saying. Usually the letters are on a black background. If the background's yellow, that means there's a narrator talking off-screen."

Cammi pulled her notebook and pen out of her backpack and pretended to jot down a few notes. Of course, she didn't need to bother. She already knew everything Anna was telling her.

"What's cool about the music channel is that they don't just give you the words to the song, see? They give you the actual notes to the music, too."

"Anna!" Sean moaned, pointing frantically to the TV. "The game!"

"Oops," Anna said. She switched back just in time for her brothers to see their team score a touchdown.

"Anna!" both boys shouted.

"This might be a good time to disappear," Anna said.

"Be sure to write in your article that she totally ruined our game," Sean called as Anna herded Cammi out of the room.

"Sorry about that," Anna said.

"I think they're great," Cammi said truthfully. "I've always wanted to have an older brother."

"Please. Take one of mine," Anna joked, leading Cammi into the kitchen, where her parents were putting up wallpaper.

"How about two for the price of one?" Anna's mother said, catching the tail end of their conversation.

"Better yet, *we'll* pay *you*!" Anna's father added. As both of them spoke, they used sign language, just as Anna's brothers had done.

"Mom and Dad, this is Cammi Adams," Anna said. "Watch out," she added to Cammi. "They're dangerous when they get involved in home improvements."

"Nice to meet you," Mrs. Reynolds said with

a smile as she struggled with a wet strip of wallpaper. She set it aside so she could sign more easily. "I don't suppose you have any experience in this field, do you?"

"Well, no," Cammi said shyly. "I'm more of a journalist, actually."

Mrs. Reynolds laughed. "You'd better go hide out in your room, Anna, before we glue you both to the wall."

Anna led the way upstairs. "Oh, by the way," she said, pausing in the hall outside her bedroom. "That's a TDD next to the phone there. It's—"

"I know," Cammi said. She bit her lip as soon as the words were out of her mouth.

"I guess you've already been doing some research, huh?"

"A little," Cammi said, looking away.

"They're great machines," Anna said. "I wish everyone had them."

Cammi stared at Anna in surprise. She didn't seem to mind showing off these gadgets. In fact, Anna almost seemed to assume that Cammi would find them interesting.

"I was wondering," Cammi said as she entered Anna's bright yellow room. "Does your family always sign at home?"

"Yep," Anna said. "Except Toby."

"Toby?"

"Our cat. I'm still working on him."

"It must be a relief for you to come home and not have to read lips," Cammi said.

Anna nodded. "I'm surprised you'd think of that. But you're right. Reading lips is really frustrating sometimes, and when I come home, it's like—" She paused, and for a moment she looked a little bit sad. "It's like I'm with people from the same country, you know? We all speak the same language."

"Why would you want to come to Sweet Valley Middle School, then?" Cammi asked bluntly.

"Simple," Anna said with a grin. "I want to go to a regular school and be treated like a regular person."

But you never will be, Cammi wanted to say. Instead she wrote down Anna's words in her notebook.

"Sorry my room's such a disaster," Anna said as she cleared away some clothes on her bed to make room for Cammi to sit down. "I went to the Wakefields' beach party yesterday, and it must have taken me five hours to decide what to wear." She sat down on the floor, legs crossed. "I'm sorry you couldn't make it. Elizabeth told me you had to baby-sit."

Cammi nodded.

"It was a great party. And I met the most incredibly cute, wonderful, amazing guy! Don't write that down, by the way. I wouldn't want to scare him off."

"Who is it?" Cammi asked, sitting stiffly on the edge of the bed.

"Jim Sturbridge," Anna said. "Do you know him?"

"I know who he is."

"Isn't he the cutest guy you've ever met?" Anna asked, closing her eyes and sighing. "Never mind that," she added, her eyes flying open. "He's mine, all mine!" She giggled. "At least I hope so."

Cammi smiled politely. *Boy-crazy*, she started to write, but suddenly her pen went dry. As she reached for a pen on Anna's desk, she noticed a copy of the social studies quiz Mrs. Arnette had given Friday. There was a big red *F* at the top of the page. *That's funny*, Cammi thought. *I thought that quiz was a breeze.*

She looked over at Anna, who was watching her closely. "By the way, how are you doing in your classes so far?" Cammi asked.

Anna busied herself folding some of the clothing that was strewn around the carpet. "Fine," she said quickly. "Just fine. I mean, the Hairnet puts me to sleep, but otherwise—"

Cammi nodded. The quiz was probably just a fluke. Anna didn't sound as if she were having any trouble. *And besides*, Cammi added to herself ruefully, *everything else in Anna's life seems to be going perfectly.*

Cammi stared down at her notebook. Why did it all seem so easy for Anna? Within a few days, she already had lots of friends and even a cute boyfriend. Cammi tried to fight the feeling of jealousy welling up inside her. She knew Anna's popularity would fade soon enough. Still, it was amazing how well she *seemed* to be fitting in.

"So, is there anything else you want to ask?" Anna prompted. "You know—about being deaf?"

Cammi thought for a moment. "I was wondering—" She paused. "Well, I guess I was wondering how you can manage to be so happy all the time. Aren't you ever angry about being . . . different?" Cammi looked away, annoyed to feel tears welling up in her own eyes.

"I used to be," Anna replied, her face growing serious. "But one day when I was really feeling bad, one of my teachers told me I had a choice. I could sit around feeling sorry for myself, or I could open my eyes and see how lucky I really was. She said I was using my deafness as an excuse for being miserable, and you know what? She was right." She shrugged. "Still, I have my good days and my bad days, just like anybody else."

Good days and bad days, Cammi wrote in her notebook. But somehow she found it hard to believe that Anna had been having any bad days lately.

"Did you see the sign-up sheet for Anna's aerobics class on the cafeteria door?" Lila asked Jessica on Monday in the cafeteria.

Jessica didn't answer. She was busy scanning the tables, trying to locate Jake Hamilton.

"Jessica? Who are you looking for?"

Jessica spun around. "Nobody," she said quickly. So far, she'd managed to keep her secret about Jake and Cathy from the Unicorns for more than thirty-six hours. She was sure she'd set a new record for self-restraint.

"You've been acting weird all morning," Ellen commented. "And you aren't even eating your chocolate cake."

"She's still recovering from all those hot dogs she ate at the beach party," Mandy Miller teased.

"Did anyone see anything . . . strange at the beach party?" Jessica asked in what she hoped was a casual voice.

"Not unless you count Winston Egbert trying to limbo," Belinda Layton replied.

Jessica poked at her cake with her fork. "I was thinking more, uh, romantically."

"You know something, don't you?" Lila said, sitting up very straight in her chair.

"Me? No!" Jessica replied. "I don't know anything. I just wondered if anyone else knew anything I didn't know that I might like to know. If you know what I mean."

Lila crossed her arms over her chest. "Spill it, Jessica."

"Lila's right!" Ellen exclaimed. She leaned close to Jessica, peering at her. "Look at the way

Jessica's mouth is twitching. She only does that when she's lying."

Jessica swallowed hard. Her secret felt like a time bomb ticking away inside of her, ready to explode at some embarrassing moment. She could just imagine it. She'd be in the middle of English class. Mr. Bowman would ask, "Are there any other questions, class?" and she would raise her hand and burst out, "What could a sophomore like Cathy possibly see in a seventh grader like Jake?"

It would be humiliating. Better to tell the truth now in the privacy of the Unicorner. "Do you all swear that this news will never go farther than Unicorn ears?" she whispered.

Everyone nodded excitedly, leaning in close.

"Well—" Jessica began, but then her eyes fell on Lila. Poor Lila. This would break her heart. Still, wouldn't it be better to hear it from her own best friend instead of a stranger?

"It's Jake," Jessica whispered.

"*My* Jake?" Lila demanded.

Jessica nodded. "He's seeing another woman, Lila."

"What?" Lila cried as the rest of the Unicorns gasped.

"And the worst part is, it's an *older* woman."

"*How* old?" Lila cried.

"Ancient. A sophomore."

Lila leaned back in her chair in stunned silence.

"I had to tell," Jessica said to the other Unicorns. "I was afraid I'd burst."

"You did the right thing," Janet assured her.

"I don't believe it," Lila said firmly. "Jake is innocent until proven guilty."

"I saw it with my own eyes, Lila."

"You're going to have to show me some proof, Jessica. Otherwise, I'm standing by my man," Lila insisted.

"They were kissing," Jessica said. "Over on the rocks."

"Kissing?" Lila demanded.

Jessica nodded. "On the rocks."

"Who's the girl?" Lila hissed. "I want to know, so I can make her life miserable." She paused. "Or maybe I'll just make *Jake's* life miserable."

"Whatever happened to standing by your man?" Belinda asked.

"And having some proof?" Mandy added.

"I don't need proof," Lila said. "I have Jessica." She leaned across the table. "Now tell me who it was."

Jessica shook her head. "If I told you, it might hurt a certain innocent person who shall remain nameless." Whatever she did, she couldn't risk humiliating her own brother.

"*Who* shall remain nameless?" Ellen asked.

"Both of them," Jessica said. "The hurter and the—the hurtee." She wasn't exactly sure that was a word, but it sounded good.

"But I'm the biggest hurtee of all," Lila moaned. Then her face turned angry. "That is, until I get hold of the hurter. Then *he'll* be the one who's hurting!"

Jessica let out a long breath. She felt better already. Some secrets just had to be told. And if she couldn't trust the Unicorns, whom could she trust?

Seven

◇

"Here it is," Cammi said to Elizabeth, meeting her in the hallway on Monday afternoon. "The profile on Anna." She started to walk away, but Elizabeth touched her elbow.

"Wait," she said. "Let me glance over it before you go. I can't wait to read it."

Cammi leaned against her locker and sighed. She had a feeling Elizabeth wasn't going to be happy with what she'd written, and she hated to let her down. But it was the best she could do under the circumstances.

Elizabeth scanned the carefully handwritten page. At first she furrowed her brow, as though she were confused. When she got to the bottom of the page, she looked up at Cammi. "Is there another page?" she asked.

"No," Cammi said softly. "That's it."

"It's kind of short, isn't it?" Elizabeth said. "I mean, what you've done looks really good. I was just hoping you'd talk to Anna more about what it's like to be deaf. Don't you think people would be interested in knowing more about things like sign language?"

Cammi studied her fingernails, avoiding Elizabeth's eyes. "Well, to tell you the truth, Elizabeth," she said, "Anna didn't seem to want to talk about it very much." *And neither did I*, Cammi added to herself.

"Are we talking about the same Anna?" Elizabeth said with a laugh.

"I'm sorry you don't like the article," Cammi said quietly.

"It's not that, Cammi," Elizabeth said quickly. "But maybe you could talk to Anna again. She was hoping this article would help the rest of us know how to act around deaf people. Anna says people are sometimes uncomfortable at first, you know?"

"I know," Cammi replied evenly. *Do I ever.* "But to tell you the truth, I just don't have time to work on this article anymore. I'm really swamped with homework. Maybe you should get Julie or Amy to give it a try. They'd probably do a much better job."

Elizabeth stared at Cammi doubtfully. "Is anything bothering you?" she asked gently.

"I'm fine," Cammi said, forcing herself to

smile. "And really, I'm sorry I did such a lousy job on that profile. I guess Anna and I just couldn't find much to talk about."

Before Elizabeth could ask any more questions, Cammi ran off down the hallway. When Elizabeth called her name, Cammi just pretended she hadn't heard.

"How's the *Sixers* coming this week?" Mr. Bowman asked that afternoon after school.

Elizabeth looked up from the photocopy machine. "Fine," she said, "except that this machine keeps eating all our paper."

"Let me have a look," Mr. Bowman said. He knelt down and opened up the side of the machine. "Just as I thought," he said, pulling out a crumpled piece of paper. "It's having digestive problems again."

"There's one other problem," Elizabeth said. "Nothing major, or anything. I've just decided not to print Cammi's interview with Anna Reynolds. At least, not in this issue."

"Why's that?" Mr. Bowman asked as he stood up. "Cammi always does wonderful interviews."

Elizabeth hesitated. She was worried about Cammi, but she wasn't sure she had anything to tell Mr. Bowman yet. "It was just that the article was a little short," Elizabeth said finally. "We can print it another time."

"That's OK with me," Mr. Bowman said. He

turned to leave. "And by the way, keep an eye on that contraption. I heard a rumor that it tried to eat Mr. Nydick's tie last week."

Elizabeth laughed as she watched Mr. Bowman head out into the hall. He was such a great teacher. Maybe she should have tried to talk to him about Cammi. But what could she have said? She wasn't even sure what was wrong.

Still, something about the interview with Anna had upset Cammi—Elizabeth was sure of that much. She couldn't help feeling responsible, since she was the one who'd assigned the interview to begin with.

It looked as though Elizabeth was going to have to do a little interviewing herself—but it wasn't Anna she needed to talk to. It was Cammi.

"I hope we're not too late for Anna's aerobics class," Amy said. It was Tuesday afternoon, and she and Elizabeth were rushing toward the gym.

"I told her we'd be a little late," Elizabeth said. "She knows we had to wrap up the *Sixers* this afternoon."

They turned the corner and dashed through the empty lobby. "By the way, where was Cammi today?" Amy asked. "I thought she was going to help us staple the papers together."

"She said she had too much homework," Elizabeth replied. She paused. "You haven't noticed anything different about her lately, have you?"

"Now that you mention it, she *has* seemed especially quiet—" Suddenly Amy stopped in midstride and grabbed Elizabeth's arm. "Look," she whispered.

There, in front of the gym door, were Anna and Mr. Clark. Anna looked upset, and Mr. Clark was shaking his head as he spoke.

"I wonder if something's wrong," Elizabeth whispered.

"Maybe she forgot to get permission to use the gym," Amy suggested.

"Let's wait here," Elizabeth said. "I don't want to interrupt."

After a few moments Mr. Clark turned back down the hall, leaving Anna standing alone by the doors. She was holding a large portable cassette player.

"Hello, ladies," Mr. Clark said as he passed Amy and Elizabeth. "Better hurry! That gym is pretty full."

Elizabeth looked at Amy. "I guess everything's OK."

When Anna saw them approaching, she took a deep breath and smiled. "Ready for a workout?" she called out.

Amy nodded. "What did Mr. Clark want?"

Anna turned away and reached for the door. "Oh, nothing," she said quickly. "He was just giving me a little pep talk, telling me to keep up the good work." She nodded toward the gym. "Come on. Let's dance!"

Amy and Elizabeth followed Anna inside. There were nearly two dozen kids there, dressed in leotards or shorts and T-shirts. Some were already stretching out, while others were sitting on the bleachers, waiting. Elizabeth waved to Jessica, who was sitting on a mat in her bright-purple leggings doing calf stretches.

"It's about time," Lila shouted. "Ellen needs emergency calorie burning after the lunch she ate."

"*I'm* not the one who had three servings of chocolate pudding," Ellen retorted.

"Trust me," Anna said. "You're all going to burn plenty of calories before we're through. Come on, everybody." She clapped her hands. "Let's get going."

Elizabeth watched Anna as she set the cassette player on the floor and popped in a tape. Somehow, she didn't seem quite as enthusiastic as Elizabeth had expected. Maybe she was a little nervous about leading such a big class—especially when everyone could hear except her.

Anna punched the *play* button and moved to the center of the gym. "Here we go," she said. As music boomed out of the cassette player, Anna moved gracefully to the beat in perfect rhythm, and Elizabeth instantly stopped worrying about her.

"Let's start with some simple steps," Anna yelled to the group.

Maybe the steps were simple for Anna, Elizabeth thought two songs later as she stumbled over her own feet for the fifteenth time, but for Elizabeth they were practically impossible. She looked over at Amy for moral support. Unfortunately, Amy had just tripped and landed on the floor in a heap.

"I'm not sure if the rest of my body's going to get a workout," Amy told Elizabeth ruefully as she clambered to her feet. "But I'm sure my rear end will!"

"I thought this was supposed to be fun," Lila complained loudly. "I'll probably never be able to walk again."

"I guess this is what you call real exercise," Jessica said, panting as she wiped her brow with a towel.

"Who wants real exercise?" Janet demanded. "All I wanted to do was show everyone how great I looked in my new leotard."

"What a bunch of weaklings," Belinda joked. "That was an easy workout. But I'm sure Anna will build up to more serious stuff later, after you wimps get used to it."

"Hey, at least I kept up," Jessica pointed out. "Ellen kept stopping during the lunges."

"I wasn't stopping on purpose," Ellen protested. "I just couldn't keep track of which leg we were lunging with."

"Tired?" Anna asked as she walked by.

"They're exhausted," Belinda replied.

"You were right, Anna," Jessica said. "About being a great dancer." She grinned. "Maybe you're a little *too* great, if you know what I mean."

"Sorry," Anna said. "I'll slow down a little next time."

"Same time next week?" Jessica asked.

Anna looked away, frowning. "Let's wait and see," she said. "I'll have to check with Mr. Clark."

"About using the gym?" Lila asked, but Anna walked away without answering.

"She probably didn't catch what you asked," Jessica said.

From the far end of the gym, there was a sudden outburst of noise as a dozen guys came bounding in from the boys' locker room.

"Great," Janet moaned. "Here comes the entire guys' basketball team, and I'm covered with sweat."

"You girls worn out by a little aerobics?" Rick teased as he walked by.

"We had a tough workout," Jessica said defensively.

Rick headed down the court and passed the ball to Jake, who made an easy lay-up.

Jessica looked over and saw that Lila's eyes were boring into Jake like laser beams. "He looks so sweet and innocent," Lila muttered. "You'd never know he was a two-timing jerk."

On his way back up the court, Jake smiled and waved at Lila. She scowled, and he lost his concentration. The ball bounced toward the bleachers, where Belinda caught it. "Here, Jake," she said, throwing it back to him.

"What are you doing, Hamilton?" Peter Jeffries teased. "Playing with the girls' team?"

Jake cast a glance in Lila's direction. "They're prettier than you are," he said to Peter.

"I didn't think you paid any attention to girls your own age," Peter said, waggling his eyebrows suggestively. Jessica gasped.

Jake stood still, dribbling the ball. "What are you talking about?" he asked Peter, frowning.

"Like you don't know?" Peter said.

"*I* don't know," Rick broke in as he joined the two boys.

"Oh, come on. I thought everyone had heard about it by now," Peter said. "It's the hottest rumor in school."

"So are you going to tell us, or do I have to guess?" Rick demanded.

Peter shrugged. "You should probably ask Hamilton."

"He should?" Jake asked, looking confused.

"Fine. Play dumb if you want to, but everyone else in school knows about the high-school girl who's warm for your form."

Jake's eyes went wide. "*What?*"

"Sure. And before long, we'll know her name, too," Peter said confidently. "So why don't you just go ahead and tell us now? Is it someone we know?"

Jessica spun around, glaring at her fellow Unicorns. Obviously, someone had blabbed her secret, but they were all too busy eavesdropping even to notice her dirty looks.

"Well, it wouldn't be right for *me* to tell you who the girl is," Jake said slowly. "You know, she has her reputation to consider. After all, some high-school kids might not understand what she's doing with a younger guy."

Peter laughed. "Personally, I don't get it, either."

"Excuse me," Rick interrupted, "but are we going to play basketball, or are we going to stand around gossiping about Jake's love life all day?"

As the boys headed down to the far end of the court, Jessica turned to the Unicorns. "Nobody moves!" she snapped. "Not until I find out who blabbed."

Janet shook her head impatiently. "Grow up, Jessica. You know there aren't any secrets at Sweet Valley Middle School. Anyway, it's not my fault. The person *I* told is very discreet."

"Janet's right," Ellen agreed. "Sooner or later it all comes out. Besides, I only told one person, and I swore her to secrecy."

"Yeah, and I only told two people, but I swore them to double secrecy and made them cross their hearts," Kimberly said.

Jessica rolled her eyes. "I swore all of *you* to secrecy, too. Look what good that did."

"You didn't make us cross our hearts," Ellen pointed out.

"OK, how many of you told someone?" Jessica demanded.

One by one, the Unicorns all looked away sheepishly.

"Maybe I should put it this way. Did any of you *not* tell someone?"

Mandy held up her hand. "I didn't."

"At least one of you can be trusted," Jessica said.

"Actually, Jessica, I *tried* to tell," Mandy admitted sheepishly. "But I couldn't find anyone who didn't already know."

Eight

◆

Wednesday during lunch, Jessica slid into the cafeteria line right behind Jake. "Don't turn around," she said under her breath. "It's me, Jessica."

"Hey, Jessica, what's up?" Jake said, turning his head.

"I said don't turn around!" Jessica said frantically. "I don't want the Unicorns to know I've been talking to you. Otherwise they'll cross-examine me, and in ten minutes it'll be all over the school."

Jake looked puzzled, but he turned his back to Jessica again. "All right, what do you want to talk about?" he asked over his shoulder.

"I need to know something, Jake," Jessica whispered, staring intently at the mystery meat the cafeteria servers were dishing out.

"What?" Jake whispered back.

"I need to know how serious this is."

"How serious what is?"

"You know."

"Is this about that high-school girl who's supposedly hot for me?" Jake asked, sounding a little tired.

"What else would it be about?" Jessica said impatiently. "I need to know, so I can decide on my next move."

Jake sighed. "Jessica, would you believe I have no idea what any of this is about?"

"No, I wouldn't. And there's no point in trying to be noble to keep Cathy out of this. I already know."

"Cathy?"

"Don't play dumb, Jake."

Jake shuffled forward with the line. "Cathy who? I know a lot of Cathys."

"Fine, if you want to play games. But you don't fool me for one minute. I know all about you two."

"I wish *I* did," Jake said wistfully.

"And I used to think Cathy was a really nice girl," Jessica muttered.

"*Which* Cathy?" Jake demanded. "I can't stand the suspense anymore. Which Cathy are you talking about?"

"Cathy Connors, like you don't know."

"Cathy Connors?" Jake repeated slowly. "But she's going out with your brother!"

"Why do you think I'm asking you how serious it is?" Jessica snapped.

"Cathy Connors," Jake said again, a slow smile spreading across his face. "She's really cute. For someone so much older, anyway. Still, it *is* kind of hard to believe."

"Tell me about it," Jessica exclaimed. "What could she possibly see in a seventh grader?"

Jake turned to her and shrugged helplessly. "I honestly don't know."

Cammi lay on her bed Wednesday after school, scanning the latest edition of the *Sixers*. It was a little shorter than usual, and she knew it was her fault. Elizabeth hadn't had time to fill the space where the interview with Anna should have gone.

The doorbell rang, and in the upstairs hallway the lights blinked to signal her parents. Cammi sighed. She was the only one home. Mrs. Adams was picking Cara up from her ballet lesson, and Mr. Adams was still at work.

She ran downstairs and peeked through the living room window to see who was at the door. To her horror, there, waiting patiently, was Elizabeth Wakefield.

Cammi jumped back, her heart pounding wildly. She couldn't let Elizabeth in. What if her mother came home while Elizabeth was there? Cammi wished she could pretend no one was home, but she was afraid that Elizabeth had seen her peeking through the window.

The doorbell rang again. Overhead, the lights blinked. "Cammi?" Elizabeth called.

Elizabeth *had* seen her. Cammi was sure of it. *Think quickly*, she told herself.

Slowly she pulled open the door, her hands trembling. "Elizabeth!" she exclaimed.

"Hi," Elizabeth said, taking a step forward. "I was wondering if we could talk for a few minutes."

"Um, listen, Elizabeth, I'd invite you in, but my sister has chicken pox, and I wouldn't want to expose you," Cammi lied. She wondered if Elizabeth could hear the tension in her voice.

"That's OK," Elizabeth said, reaching for the screen door. "I had chicken pox a long time ago."

Cammi grabbed the inside handle of the screen door and pulled. "Well, uh, I don't know—"

"Is it just my imagination," Elizabeth asked with a grin, "or are we playing tug-of-war with the screen door?"

At last Cammi relented. Her only hope was to get rid of Elizabeth quickly, before Mrs. Adams returned. "OK," Cammi said, holding open the door. "But just for a second. My mom went to get some medicine for Cara, and she'll be back soon. She'll probably be mad if she finds out I let you in."

"I guess I should have called," Elizabeth said

as she set her backpack on the couch, "but to tell you the truth, I was afraid you'd say you didn't feel like talking."

"Talking about what?" Cammi asked, sneaking an anxious glance at the telephone. One ring, and she'd have an awful lot of explaining to do.

"Well, for starters, the interview with Anna."

Cammi swallowed past a huge lump in her throat. "Why don't we go upstairs?" she urged. "I'll show you my bedroom."

"Great," Elizabeth said. Ludwig waddled over and sniffed her shoe. "Hi there," she said, bending over to give him a pat.

"Don't mind Ludwig," Cammi said. "He's a little senile."

"Ludwig?" Elizabeth asked.

"My parents named him after Ludwig van Beethoven."

"Is he their favorite composer?" Elizabeth said.

"Something like that," Cammi answered uncomfortably. The truth was, they'd chosen the name because Beethoven went deaf in his later years.

Cammi was halfway up the stairs when she noticed that Elizabeth had stopped and was staring at the telephone. "What kind of phone is this?" Elizabeth asked, pointing to the TDD screen.

"That?" Cammi said in a squeaky voice. "Um, would you believe that's our Bat Phone?"

Elizabeth laughed. "I had a feeling you were leading a double life, Cammi."

"Actually, that's my dad's phone," Cammi said. "He uses it for business."

"What does your dad do?"

"Dad?" Cammi cleared her throat. All of this lying was getting harder and harder by the second. "He's a, um, an inventor. He's still trying to work out the kinks in that phone."

"Cool," Elizabeth said. "I didn't know your dad—" Just then the phone rang. Cammi felt her heart drop like a stone.

"Is anything wrong with the electricity?" Elizabeth asked, staring up at the flickering light overhead.

"See what I mean about kinks?" Cammi asked. "Every time someone calls, the lights freak out."

"Aren't you going to answer it?"

"The answering machine will get it," Cammi replied. "At least *that* works."

Quickly Cammi led Elizabeth upstairs into the safety of her bedroom. Was Elizabeth staring at her a little strangely? Cammi crossed her fingers and closed the door. She'd just have to hope for the best.

"So what was it you wanted to talk about, Elizabeth?" she asked as casually as she could manage. "Something about Anna?"

"Cammi, maybe it's none of my business," Elizabeth began, "but I have a feeling something's been bothering you. I thought maybe you could use a friend to talk to."

"A friend?" Cammi repeated.

Elizabeth grinned. "Me, of course."

Cammi stared doubtfully at Elizabeth. She'd always been so nice. Maybe she really could be trusted with the truth about Mr. and Mrs. Adams.

"I might not be able to help," Elizabeth added, "but I am a good listener."

Cammi chewed on her lower lip. She wanted to trust Elizabeth, but it was too risky. She couldn't bear to be laughed at, not again—

"Cammi?"

Cammi gasped. Cara was home!

"Was that your little sister?" Elizabeth asked. "I'd love to meet her."

"She shouldn't be out of bed," Cammi said. "She's probably delirious or something."

She ran to the door and eased it open, hoping to slip into the hall and somehow warn Cara and Mrs. Adams to stay away. But before she could stop her, Cara flung open the door and pirouetted in dressed in her pink leotard and tutu.

"Look! I'm the Sugar Plum Fairy," Cara cried, spinning across Cammi's bedroom.

"What did I tell you?" Cammi said, grabbing her sister and herding her toward the door. "She's hallucinating."

Elizabeth cocked her head to one side, grinning. "It looks to me like she's recovering pretty well."

"Who are you?" Cara demanded, finally noticing Elizabeth. She gazed up at Cammi. "Is she your friend, Cammi? I thought you didn't want any friends over—"

"Back to bed, Cara," Cammi said firmly, placing her hand on Cara's forehead. "You're burning up."

She dragged Cara down the hall by her tutu and was just about to stuff her into the bathroom when she heard Elizabeth's voice.

"Hi," Elizabeth said. "I'm Elizabeth Wakefield. You must be Cammi's mom."

Cammi didn't even bother to turn around. She closed her eyes and sighed. It was all over now. Elizabeth knew her secret.

"Won't you stay for dinner?" Mrs. Adams asked. She spoke slowly, struggling to make each word as distinct as possible.

Cammi knew that her mother's speech was difficult for most people to understand. She waited, every muscle in her body tense, for the sound of Elizabeth's laughter.

But to Cammi's surprise, Elizabeth didn't laugh. In fact, Cammi heard her say the most surprising thing of all.

"I'd love to stay," Elizabeth said. "I'll go call my mom to make sure it's all right."

"I love your parents," Elizabeth said after dinner, when she and Cammi had returned to Cammi's bedroom. "They're so nice, Cammi."

Cammi shook her head, feeling almost numb. Dinner had been wonderful. After a while, Cammi had actually forgotten to be self-conscious about her parents, and Elizabeth had almost seemed like part of the family. She'd even learned a few basic signs.

"I guess I would have invited you over a long time ago," Cammi said, "if I'd known."

"Known what?"

"That you wouldn't—" She paused. "You know, laugh at them."

"Is that why you've never told anybody that your parents are deaf?"

Cammi nodded.

"But, Cammi, you can't keep them a secret forever," Elizabeth said gently. "You'd be surprised at how accepting people are if you give them a chance. Look at how well Anna's doing."

"Anna's just been lucky so far," Cammi said with a shrug. "My guess is it won't last. People still think it's fun to know a deaf person—it's like a freak show for them. But the newness will wear off. Anna will never be able to fit in, not really."

"How can you be so sure of that?"

Cammi sighed. "Not everybody's as nice as you are, Elizabeth," she said. "I remember when I was younger, before we moved to Sweet Valley—"

Elizabeth sat down next to her on the bed. "What happened?"

"We were having Parents' Night at school,

you know? And I guess I was too little or too stupid to realize how the other kids would react when they saw my parents for the first time. It was bad enough, the way they all gawked when my mom and dad and I were signing, but then my dad raised his hand to ask the teacher a question." Cammi gulped back a sob. "You know how he doesn't speak all that clearly?"

Elizabeth nodded.

"Well, half the room just burst into laughter, Elizabeth. Not just the kids, either. Even some of the adults were laughing. It was horrible. The worst part was the way my dad reacted. He didn't feel bad because they were laughing at him —he was used to that. He felt bad because he'd embarrassed *me*. He had tears in his eyes, Elizabeth," Cammi whispered. "It's the only time I've ever seen my dad cry."

"It must have been awful for you," Elizabeth said softly.

"And the worst part was," Cammi admitted, "I felt sorry for my mom and dad, but I felt angry at them, too. I didn't understand why they couldn't just be like other parents. And then I felt guilty for being angry at them."

"But you can't hide forever, Cammi," Elizabeth said. "Sure, some kids are mean, but lots of others aren't. Look at Anna. She has to face the possibility that she'll be rejected every single day."

"And she will be."

Elizabeth shook her head. "I hope not."

"Anyway, Anna's braver than I am."

"I just think she's had more practice dealing with people than you have. Maybe if you talked to her some more—"

"No," Cammi said firmly. "I'm not ready to be like Anna. I can't risk it. It's not just me I have to worry about. It's my mom and dad, too."

"Just think about it, OK?"

"I *have* thought about it," Cammi replied. "Plenty. And nothing's going to change my mind. Nothing."

"Spill it, Elizabeth," Jessica said that evening when Elizabeth got home. "Where were you *really*?"

"I had dinner at Cammi Adams' house."

Jessica shook her head and sighed. "I know that's what you told Mom, but you can tell me the truth."

"I *am* telling you the truth," Elizabeth replied. "And since you're so interested, I had a great time. Cammi and her family are really nice."

Jessica rolled her eyes. "Cammi? Cammi *Adams*? Are you having some kind of nervous breakdown, Elizabeth? Why would you want to spend an entire evening with someone like Cammi?"

Elizabeth shot her sister a look of annoyance. "Maybe you should try giving Cammi a chance sometime. You said the same thing about Anna, and look how wrong you were. Did it ever cross your mind that maybe there's a good reason Cammi's so shy?"

"Like what?"

"Like—" Elizabeth caught herself just in time. "Forget it, Jess."

"If you say so."

Elizabeth turned to leave.

"Wait a sec," Jessica said. "I want to get your opinion about something." She flipped through the pages of a large book, then stopped.

"That's Steven's yearbook, isn't it?" Elizabeth asked. "What are you doing? Shopping around in case things don't work out with Rick?"

"Very funny. Actually, I'm shopping around for Steven."

"For *Steven*?"

"Here." Jessica held up the yearbook and pointed to a picture of a pretty dark-haired girl. "What do you think? Her name's Nicole Martin, and she's a member of the National Honor Society and a cheerleader. Beauty and brains."

Elizabeth frowned. "You know her?"

"No, of course I don't know her. I just read the caption under her picture. But she looks like Steven's type, don't you think?"

"Let me get this straight. *You're* picking out a new girlfriend for Steven?"

"Someone's going to have to help him through this," Jessica said defensively.

"Jessica, there probably isn't even a *this* for him to work through."

"I had a talk with Jake in the cafeteria today," Jessica said. "Trust me. He had guilt written all over his face."

"I still don't believe it."

"OK," Jessica said, thumbing through the yearbook. "I get the feeling you don't like Nicole. How about this girl, Haley Rodriguez? She's got a nice smile, and she was voted Most Spirited Sophomore."

"I don't know," Elizabeth replied as she walked out the door. "But if they ever have an election for Most Insane Sixth Grader, you've got my vote for sure."

Nine

◇

"How'd you do on that English quiz?" Amy asked Elizabeth as the two girls stepped into the bathroom after class on Friday.

"Fine," Elizabeth said. She paused in front of a mirror and ran a brush through her hair. "In fact, I think I might have aced it."

Suddenly they heard a wrenching sob coming from behind one of the stall doors. Elizabeth looked at Amy in alarm. Amy pointed to a crumpled piece of paper on the floor, next to the stall where the sob had come from.

"Are you OK in there?" Elizabeth called while Amy picked up the paper and unfolded it. The only answer was another sob.

Amy passed the paper to Elizabeth. It was the quiz from Mr. Bowman's class, and at the top of the page was a large red *F*. Next to the *F* was the name Anna Reynolds.

"Anna?" Elizabeth called. Then she slapped her forehead. "Brilliant, Elizabeth. She can't hear you."

She stuck her hand up over the top of the stall door and carefully signed the letters for her name that Anna had taught her.

"Hi, Elizabeth," Anna replied, sniffling.

Elizabeth made the signs for the letters *O* and *K*.

"Yes, I'm fine," Anna said. Slowly the door to the stall opened, and Anna stepped out. Her eyes were swollen, and her cheeks were streaked with tears.

"It's just a grammar quiz," Amy said. "Don't worry about it, Anna. If you want, we could all study for the next test together."

"It wouldn't help," Anna muttered. "Nothing will."

"Lots of people hate grammar," Elizabeth pointed out with a smile.

"You don't understand." Anna turned on a faucet and splashed cold water on her face. "Or I guess I should say *I* don't understand."

"What do you mean?" Elizabeth asked.

Anna shrugged. "I can't follow any of my teachers. I'll be lipreading just fine, but then they'll turn around to write on the board or something, and I'll completely lose track of what's going on."

"Maybe if you talked to them and explained that you're having trouble," Amy suggested.

"I've tried. My parents called Mr. Clark, too. He reminded all the teachers to be careful when they're lecturing, but I guess it's hard to break old habits." She looked in the mirror, shaking her head sadly. "It's not their fault, anyway. It's mine, for being stupid enough to think I could ever fit in at a regular school."

"Anna, don't say that," Elizabeth cried, but as she spoke she remembered Cammi's prediction that Anna wouldn't last. Maybe Cammi had been right after all.

Anna reached for her crumpled quiz and tossed it in the wastebasket.

"Maybe Mr. Bowman will let you take a make-up quiz," Amy said. "We could really help you cram this weekend—"

"But what about the next quiz?" Anna asked. "And the next? This morning Mr. Clark told me that if things don't improve in the next week or so, maybe I should reconsider my decision to come here."

"But you just got here!" Elizabeth said. "They're not giving you enough time."

"I don't want to be treated differently, Elizabeth," Anna said firmly. "If I can't make it, I can't make it. Besides, Mr. Clark's not trying to be mean. He just doesn't want me to fall too far behind. He had his doubts about my coming here to begin with, and now he's really worried. I used to get straight *As* at my other school.''

"Still," Amy said, "we'd all really miss you, Anna.''

Anna's chin began to quiver. "I'd miss you guys, too. And my aerobics class. And Jim.'' She bit her lip to keep from crying. "Look," she whispered. "Just do me a favor, OK?''

"Anything," Elizabeth promised.

Anna straightened her shoulders and took a deep breath. "Just don't feel sorry for me, whatever happens. That's the only thing I can't stand.''

"Great!" Steven said, slamming down the phone Friday after dinner.

"What's the matter?" Jessica asked, looking up from the magazine she was reading.

Steven gave her a sour look. "I don't know why you're being so nice to me lately, but whatever it is, I'm not falling for it.''

"I just wanted to know why you were upset, that's all," Jessica said.

"Cathy canceled our date tonight. There. Are you satisfied?''

"She canceled your date?" Jessica repeated angrily. *It's starting already*, she thought. *Cathy's probably meeting Jake instead.*

Steven shrugged. "She's spending the weekend at her aunt's, and she had to pack tonight.''

"Oh, *sure*," Jessica said, throwing her magazine down.

"They're leaving early tomorrow morning," Steven explained, giving Jessica a puzzled look.

"And you believe that?" Jessica demanded. "Boys are so gullible."

"Why shouldn't I believe it? Cathy wouldn't lie to me."

"She wouldn't, huh?" Jessica asked. This was the perfect opportunity to introduce Steven to the idea that Cathy might not be what she seemed. "Maybe you should stop being so naive and trusting," she advised. "Some women can be very tricky."

"Right. Whatever you say, Jessica," Steven said, waving his hand dismissively.

Jessica decided that she was going to have to be a little more direct. "I'm sure Cathy is capable of lying to you," she said.

"No, she's not," Steven said confidently. "I'd know."

"You'd be the *last* to know." Jessica shook her head sadly.

"Why would Cathy come up with some story to get out of our date?" Steven asked. "We were going to a movie that she's been dying to see. It's some dumb love story. *I'm* the one who didn't want to go see it."

Jessica sighed. *Poor Steven. Of course Cathy didn't want to go see a love story—not with the boy she was betraying.*

Suddenly she had a wonderfully sneaky idea. "I guess, if she's home packing," Jessica said casually, "then she'd still be there if we called, right?"

"Uh-huh. But why would I want to call her when I just got off the phone with her?"

Jessica marched over to the phone and lifted the receiver. "Are you afraid to call her?"

"Excuse me, Jessica, but has your body been taken over by aliens or something? You've been acting even stranger than usual lately, and that's saying a lot."

"Give me the number. *I'll* call her if you're afraid to," Jessica insisted. This was the perfect opportunity to let Steven find out the truth for himself.

Steven rolled his eyes. "Thanks, but I have a life to lead, midget." He headed toward the stairs.

"Tell me her number," Jessica demanded.

Steven paused. "Fine," he said, shaking his head in bewilderment. He walked back to the phone, took it from Jessica's hand, and punched in some numbers.

"Hi, it's me," he said after a moment's wait.

So Cathy hadn't sneaked out yet. Jessica couldn't help feeling a little disappointed.

"Yeah, I know I just talked to you," Steven said, "but I'm calling to ask you something very important. Jessica has gone nuts. Would you talk her into seeking professional treatment?" He handed the phone to Jessica, grinned, and took off.

"Hello?" the voice on the line said. "Jessica?"

"Um . . . wrong number!" Jessica blurted, slamming down the phone.

Obviously, saving Steven from humiliation was going to be more complicated than she had realized.

On Saturday afternoon, Elizabeth was stretched out on a lounge chair in the Wakefields' backyard with a brand-new book by her favorite author, Amanda Howard. However, she had only gotten to page two when she heard Jessica calling her.

"Elizabeth!" Jessica cried, dashing over with Lila right behind her. "Why didn't you tell me?"

"Tell you what?" Elizabeth asked, lowering her book.

"About Anna Reynolds getting kicked out," Jessica said.

Poor Anna, Elizabeth thought sadly. *I guess the word's out already about Mr. Clark's ultimatum.* "She's not getting kicked out—not yet, that is," Elizabeth said. "Where did you hear that story, anyway?"

"From Ellen, who heard it from Mandy, who heard it from Caroline, who heard it from Jim—"

"No," Lila interrupted, "Mandy heard it from Belinda. *Belinda* heard it from Caroline."

"Never mind," Elizabeth said with a sigh. "I get the picture. The whole school knows."

"But *you* knew first," Jessica said. "At least,

that's what Caroline said. How come you didn't tell me?"

"I didn't think Anna would want anyone else to know. Besides, it wasn't very long ago that I had to practically bribe you to go meet Anna at Casey's."

"But now we're friends," Jessica said sadly, sitting down on the grass. "I can't believe this is happening. What about our aerobics class? We've got to figure out a way to help Anna."

Elizabeth shrugged. "How?"

"I don't know." Jessica rubbed her chin thoughtfully. "Maybe we could all take turns writing down what teachers say."

"I don't think that's very practical," Elizabeth said.

"Why not?" Jessica asked.

"Well, for one thing, you have lousy handwriting, Jessica," Lila pointed out.

Jessica stood, brushing the grass off her knees. "So maybe that won't work. But we'll think of something."

Elizabeth picked up her book again. "Save me some lemonade, Jess."

"How did you know I was going to make lemonade?" Jessica asked in surprise.

"I just had a feeling," Elizabeth said. "Besides, it's hot, and you're heading for the kitchen."

"Maybe you're psychic, Elizabeth," Lila teased.

Elizabeth laughed. "Just a lucky guess."

"Well, anyway," Jessica said, "keep thinking, Lizzie. There's got to be some way we can help Anna."

Elizabeth shook her head as she watched the two of them head off. If only Jessica were right.

On Monday, Cammi found she was having a hard time concentrating during English class. She stifled a yawn as she watched Mr. Bowman write a list of sentences on the board. Was there anything in the world more boring than grammar?

Next to her, she heard a strange sound. If she hadn't known better, she would have sworn that Anna was crying. Cammi pretended to drop her pencil on the floor. When she bent down to pick it up, she sneaked a glance at Anna.

Anna *was* crying. Her eyes were wet with tears, and she was holding a wadded-up tissue in her hand.

Cammi sat up quickly. As she did, she noticed Elizabeth glancing back at Anna, a worried expression on her face. *Can I help?* Elizabeth mouthed silently to Anna.

Cammi looked up at Mr. Bowman, who was lecturing away about adverbs, his back to the class as he wrote on the board.

So that was it. Anna was having trouble lip-reading.

For a moment Cammi felt a sharp pang of sympathy. She knew all too well what Anna was going through. Cammi's parents had suffered through it hundreds of times. She'd seen the frustration and hurt on their faces as they tried to keep up with a world that wouldn't wait.

Cammi knew Mr. Bowman wasn't being thoughtless. He was just teaching the way he always taught. It was hard to change old habits. She wondered if Anna was having the same problem with all her other teachers.

"And that's the amazing adverb," Mr. Bowman concluded as he erased the board. "Stay tuned for more on its fascinating friend, the action verb!"

The whole class groaned. Cammi knew that Anna must be wondering what was going on. For a moment, she almost said something, but then she stopped herself. *This isn't my problem*, she thought silently. *Anna shouldn't even be putting herself through this in the first place.*

Cammi sat there for a few more minutes, trying with all her might not to think about Anna anymore. *Forget about it*, she told herself. *There's nothing I can do.*

Anna sniffled again.

Well, maybe there was one thing Cammi could do. She grabbed her backpack and pulled out a fresh tissue.

Then, without a word, she reached across the aisle and handed it to Anna.

Ten

That afternoon, Cammi was pulling books from her locker when she overheard Caroline Pearce talking to Ellen.

"I'd cry, too," Caroline was saying, "if I were getting kicked out of school."

Cammi closed her locker quietly and kept listening. Caroline wasn't the most reliable source for news, but she was definitely the loudest.

"I don't know why she came here in the first place," Ellen said. "Mr. Clark's right. She can't keep up with regular students."

Cammi slung her backpack over one shoulder and approached Caroline. "Who's getting kicked out?" she asked casually. "Anybody I know?"

Caroline rolled her eyes. "Where have you

been, Cammi? Living in a cave? Everybody knows Anna Reynolds is history."

"You mean, she's leaving school?"

"Not yet," Caroline replied. "But she will be soon, if her grades don't improve." She tossed her long red hair over her shoulder. "If you ask me, it's for her own good. I mean, I really like Anna and everything. But why would a deaf girl think she could make it in a regular school? You know what I mean?"

"Yeah," Cammi said grimly. "I know, all right."

Cammi turned away and walked slowly down the hall, Caroline's words echoing in her ears. *What right does Caroline have to judge Anna?* she thought angrily.

Still, Cammi wasn't surprised that Anna was leaving. She'd known all along that Anna wouldn't survive. Hadn't she told Elizabeth this would happen?

Cammi pushed open the lobby door and stepped into the bright afternoon sunlight. She'd been right about Anna all along. So why did she feel so wrong inside?

"Just look at him," Lila said that afternoon, shaking her head sadly. "While Steven's down there, happily mowing the lawn, his girlfriend is busy stabbing him in the back."

Jessica joined Lila at the bedroom window and peered down. As they watched, the lawn mower engine sputtered to a stop, and Steven began yelling at it in frustration.

"I wouldn't say he's *happily* mowing the lawn," Jessica said. "It's not exactly his favorite thing to do."

"Still, his one true love is two-timing him, and he doesn't even know it." Lila sighed heavily. "Unlike me." She patted Jessica on the back. "I'm glad you finally told me, Jessica. I feel better somehow, knowing who the other woman is."

"Well, once you guessed, I figured I had to tell," Jessica said. "But you have to promise not to tell a soul." She turned to Ellen, who was sitting on Jessica's bed. "And this time I mean it!"

Ellen crossed her heart. "You can trust me, Jessica." She joined the others at the window. "Lila, since when is Jake your one true love?"

"He *could* have been my one true love," Lila said defensively. "If he weren't such a jerk."

Jessica watched Steven as he kicked the lawn mower. "You know, Elizabeth says I shouldn't say anything to Steven, but I feel like a traitor not telling him the truth."

"You *are* a traitor," Lila agreed. "He should know. It'll break his heart, of course, but he definitely should know."

"Why?" Ellen asked.

Lila gave her an exasperated look. "Because people should know what other people are doing behind their backs."

"Lila's right," Jessica said. "I want Steven to be happy."

"But if you tell him the truth, won't he be *un*happy?"

"Yes, Ellen, but it will be an honest unhappiness instead of a dishonest happiness," Jessica explained.

"Exactly." Lila nodded. "There's nothing worse than being happy when you shouldn't be."

"But how would I break it to him?" Jessica asked.

"Just come right out with it," Lila advised. "Honesty is the best policy."

Jessica shook her head. "I think I should build up to it slowly. Maybe I could start by telling him about Marston and Maggie on *Days of Turmoil*."

"I don't think so," Ellen replied. "Marston was so depressed over losing Maggie that he drove his car into a brick wall. He had to have tons of plastic surgery on his face. Now he's a totally different actor."

"Steven's too young to drive," Jessica pointed out.

She glanced out the window again. Steven had finally gotten the mower started again. He was cutting the grass that bordered the garage. This would be the perfect time to tell him. After all, he was already in a bad mood. How much worse could he feel?

"I'll do it," Jessica said decisively. "It's my

duty to tell him. Every minute I delay, it's like I'm lying to him. And I would never do that."

"Never," Lila echoed.

"How about the time—"

"Let's not dredge up ancient history, Ellen," Lila snapped.

Jessica took a deep breath. "OK. Let's go," she said, leading the way downstairs and out to the lawn.

"You're doing the right thing, Jessica," Lila said as they marched toward Steven.

"Steven!" Jessica yelled over the noise of the mower. She stood in front of him and waved her arms, but Steven just motioned for her to get out of the way. Finally, in frustration, Jessica reached over and pulled the lever that turned the mower off. The engine sputtered and died.

"Are you nuts?" Steven yelled frantically. "Do you know how hard it is to start this thing?"

"This is important, Steven," Jessica said, crossing her arms over her chest.

"Nothing involving you three can possibly be important to me," Steven said, bending down to restart the mower.

"It involves Cathy," Jessica said.

Steven hesitated, then sighed. "All right, spit it out."

"Steven, what I'm going to tell you may break your heart," Jessica warned.

"It broke mine," Lila added.

"Well, my heart was already broken once today," Steven said.

"It was?"

"Yeah. When you shut off the stupid mower," he said, glaring at Jessica.

"This is much worse, Steven," Jessica said. She put a comforting hand on her brother's shoulder, but he brushed it off.

"I'm giving you ten seconds to say whatever it is you want to say. One . . . two . . ."

"But I need to prepare you," Jessica exclaimed.

"Three . . . four . . ."

"It's not the kind of thing you just blurt out!" Jessica protested.

"Five . . . six . . ."

"Maybe you should sit down on the porch or something."

"Seven . . . eight . . ."

"Cathy's going out with another guy behind your back, and I know because I saw them kissing over in the rocks at the beach party!" Jessica shouted all in one breath.

Steven stopped counting. He stared at her for a long time, his eyes narrowed. "Who?" he asked at last.

"He's a seventh grader."

"*Who?*"

"His name is Jake. Jake Hamilton."

"He was my one true love," Lila put in helpfully.

Steven's eyes blazed. His lips trembled and twitched. Jessica took a step backward. He was taking this worse than she'd expected. She'd never seen Steven twitch before.

"I'll destroy him!" Steven cried in a strangled voice. "I'll crush him!"

"Relax, Steven. You'll find someone else. I've even picked out a few possibilities already."

Steven turned to Lila. "Where can I find this little worm?" he demanded, ignoring Jessica.

"Um, I don't know," Lila hedged, looking a little bit frightened.

"I know," Ellen said.

"Ellen—" Jessica warned, but Steven grabbed Ellen by the shoulders.

"Where?" he cried. "Where can I find the little vermin who destroyed my life?"

"He has basketball practice tomorrow afternoon at the middle-school gym."

"Basketball practice!" Steven repeated gleefully. "I'll see to it that he never, ever dribbles again!"

When Cammi got home from school, she found Cara in the front yard with a little black-haired girl Cammi had never seen before. Ludwig sat between them, patiently wagging his tail.

"This is Joan," Cara said. "My new best friend."

Cammi smiled. Little kids made friends so easily.

"Hi, Joan," she said. "I'm Cammi, Cara's big sister."

"She already knows," Cara said as she opened a package of Ludwig's favorite treats, Cat Nips. They were little bacon-flavored biscuits in the shape of cats.

Joan nodded solemnly. "I know all about you," she announced. "You let Cara try on your jewelry and you always take her to movies and you're nice, most of the time, and also very smart and very brave."

"Wow." Cammi whistled. "Cara said all that nice stuff about me?"

"Yep."

Cammi sat down on the grass next to Ludwig. "Did she also mention that I'm the most popular girl in school?" she asked with a wry smile.

"Are you?" Joan asked, wide-eyed.

"No," Cammi admitted, shaking her head. "Not exactly."

"That's OK. Being brave's more important than being popular," Joan said confidently.

"Are you sure?" Cammi asked.

Cara rolled her eyes. "Everybody knows *that*."

"Well, I'm afraid I'm not very popular *or* very brave," Cammi admitted softly. The image of Anna's sad face came back to her. *I could have helped*, she thought, *but I didn't. How's that for brave?*

Mrs. Adams came out on the porch and waved. "How was school?" she signed.

"The usual," Cammi signed back. She glanced at Cara. Was she worried about Joan seeing Mrs. Adams? Cara didn't seem to care. She was busy with Ludwig.

"I wish my mom couldn't hear," Joan said as Mrs. Adams went back inside. "I could turn up the TV as loud as I wanted."

"The radio, too," Cara confirmed.

So Cara had told Joan the truth already. *Why is it so much easier for her?* Cammi wondered. Maybe, like Anna, she'd just had better luck so far. Or maybe, Cammi thought with a grim smile, Cara just called the mean kids booger-heads and went on about her business.

"Would you teach me to finger talk, too?" Joan asked as she stroked Ludwig's head.

Cara pursed her lips. "It's hard work," she said seriously.

"I can learn," Joan promised.

"OK, but first we do Ludwig."

"What exactly are you doing to Ludwig?" Cammi asked as she lay back on the grass.

"Teaching him to speak," Cara answered.

"Cara," Cammi said, shaking her head. "Give it up. We've tried that a million times."

"How come?" Joan asked.

Cammi sighed. She hated explaining this. It was just one more way her family was different. "It's kind of complicated, Joan," she said.

"No, it's not," Cara said casually as she reached into the box of Cat Nips. "It's easy. Ludwig doesn't bark because he grew up with my mom and dad. Since they can't hear, he figured, why bother barking?"

"Cool," Joan said, leaning over to kiss Ludwig on the muzzle. Ludwig groaned.

"And then," Cara continued, "Ludwig went to a special place called Hearing Dog School. That's why he wears this special orange collar. He's a college graduate, right, Ludwig?"

Ludwig flopped his tail, his eyes trained on the box of Cat Nips.

"Like a seeing-eye dog for blind people?" Joan asked.

"Sort of. Only Ludwig does other things. Like when we were babies and we'd cry, he would go to my mom and push her hand. Or if the phone rings, or someone's at the door—"

"He sure is smart," Joan said.

"I know. If only he could talk."

"Haven't you ever heard the expression 'you can't teach an old dog new tricks'?" Cammi asked.

"If he can learn to sign, he can learn to bark," Cara said firmly as she dangled a Cat Nip in front of Ludwig's nose.

"He knows how to finger talk?" Joan asked in surprise.

"Sure. He knows all kinds of signs. Sit, stay, all that stuff."

"Ludwig, you're wonderful," Joan said.

"Speak, Ludwig," Cara commanded. "Arf."

Ludwig wagged his tail. Cara dropped a Cat Nip in his mouth, and Ludwig crunched away gratefully. "He's trying," she explained. "It's not easy trying to talk like a regular dog after all this time."

Cammi stood and headed toward the house. "Good luck, you two."

On the porch, she paused and looked back at the two little girls. It amazed her how easily Joan accepted everything about her new friend—a mother who talked with her hands, phones that lit up, a dog that didn't bark.

She remembered what Elizabeth had said that evening she'd stayed for dinner. *Some kids are mean, but lots of others aren't.* Maybe she had a point.

Mrs. Adams came back out onto the porch. "Anything wrong?" she signed.

"I was just thinking," Cammi signed back, her index finger circling her brow.

"Before you got home, Cara was bragging about you to Joan," Mrs. Adams said.

"I know," Cammi signed. "For some reason, she was telling Joan that I was brave. What was that all about?"

"Well, I couldn't see all of the conversation clearly, but I think it had something to do with how you weren't afraid to get shots at the doctor's office."

Cammi rolled her eyes. "I figured it was something like that."

Mrs. Adams put her arm around Cammi's shoulders. "I think you're brave, too, Cammi."

"But why?" Cammi signed.

Mrs. Adams sighed. "Because you've had to grow up faster than most kids. You've had to deal with a problem other kids don't have to deal with."

"It's no problem," Cammi signed back.

"Cammi, I know what it's like to be different," Mrs. Adams signed, a gentle smile on her face. "You've handled it well, and I'm proud of you."

Cammi looked away. Her little sister thought she was brave. Her mother was proud of her. It should have made her feel wonderful. But inside she knew she didn't deserve their praise.

Cammi headed upstairs and started to work on her homework. But as hard as she tried, she couldn't seem to concentrate. After an hour of staring at her social studies textbook, she stood to stretch. Outside in the front yard, she could hear Cara and Joan, still hard at work on Ludwig's speech lessons.

She walked over to her bedroom window and pulled back the curtain—just in time to see Ludwig sit up on his hind legs and let out a mighty bark.

Eleven

◆

"Today, as promised, we're going to spend the hour getting acquainted with the fascinating world of action verbs," Mr. Bowman announced the next day as English class began.

Several people groaned.

"Hey, come on. Action verbs are a lot more fun than some other parts of speech I could mention," Mr. Bowman chided, adjusting his bow tie. "These are the verbs that really *do* things—the ones that get out in the world and have a good time. You know what I mean—*run, laugh, sing.*" He turned to the board and began writing a list of sentences. "Now, here are some examples of action verbs in action."

Cammi shifted uncomfortably in her seat. Mr. Bowman was facing the board again. She knew Anna would be missing everything he was saying.

Just then Mr. Clark appeared in the doorway. He and Mr. Bowman exchanged nods, and Mr. Clark stepped quickly to the back row, where he took a seat. Without a word, he opened up the notebook he was carrying and retrieved a pencil from his shirt pocket.

Cammi sneaked a peek in his direction. He was staring right at Anna. Obviously, Mr. Clark was here to observe how Anna was doing in the class.

"I *leap* across the chasm," Mr. Bowman read out loud as he wrote. "You *throw* the ball through the window. We *climb* over the fence."

Out of the corner of her eye, Cammi checked on Anna. Anna was sitting very still, her eyes glued to Mr. Bowman, her brow furrowed in concentration. Cammi had seen that same intense look on her parents' faces many times. Anna was waiting for him to turn back, waiting to see his lips move, so that she could try to pick up a few words and figure out what he was saying.

But Mr. Bowman kept his back to the class as he gazed at the blackboard. He waved his hand at the three sentences he had just written and asked, "Now, who can tell me what these sentences all have in common?" Finally he turned around.

"Anna?" he asked, speaking clearly and directly to her. "Do you have the answer?"

Cammi could tell he was trying to be nice.

Mr. Bowman had spoken to Anna in just the right way, hoping to make it easy for her to follow. Unfortunately, Mr. Bowman didn't realize that Anna had no idea what his original question had been.

Cammi looked over at Anna just in time to see her turn red and slump down in her seat.

"Well, um—" Anna said softly.

Mr. Clark looked down at his notebook and began scribbling. Everyone else was watching Anna. The whole class seemed to be holding its breath. A strange, eerie silence filled the room.

It was the same silence, Cammi knew, that her parents had to endure every moment of their lives. It was the silence Anna lived with, too. No wonder she wanted to pretend to be like everyone else, to leave that world behind for just a little while each day.

"I'm not sure," Anna said, her eyes brimming with tears.

Cammi scanned the room. Several kids were shifting uncomfortably in their seats. Amy and Elizabeth had both raised their hands to answer the question, probably trying to take the pressure off Anna. Ellen and Lila were whispering to each other.

It was inevitable, Cammi told herself. Already the other kids were becoming impatient with Anna. Right now they felt sorry for her, but that would change. Soon they'd start to exclude

122

Anna because she made them uncomfortable. Because she was different.

Anna should have known this would happen. She should have known that in the end no one could help her.

Cammi closed her eyes. There was one person in the room who could help Anna. But if Cammi helped now, her secret would be out forever. She'd be even more of an outsider than she already was.

"Perhaps we should give someone else a try," Mr. Bowman said gently.

Slowly Cammi opened her eyes. Maybe it was time for a little of that bravery Cara and her mom had talked about. She reached over and touched Anna's shoulder. Anna looked at her questioningly as a tear spilled down her cheek. Cammi could feel every eye in the room on her. She took a deep breath.

Then she held out her hands, and with quick, silent fingers, began to speak.

When class was over, everyone gathered around Cammi and Anna in the hallway. "Where did you learn to sign so well?" Anna asked in amazement. "You're as good as I am."

"Well," Cammi said slowly. She gazed around at the faces watching her. "Both my parents are deaf."

She waited, holding her breath. A few people

looked surprised, some others nodded, and Elizabeth smiled at her. But no one laughed.

"Well, thanks a lot for the help," Anna said. Her voice was casual, but as she spoke, she signed a separate message. "Why keep it a secret?" she asked with her hands.

"It's no big deal," Cammi said with a shrug. But just as Anna had done, her hands sent a different message. "I was afraid," she signed.

Anna nodded sadly. "I understand," she signed back.

"So does this mean maybe you can stay, now that you have Cammi to help you?" Lila asked Anna. "I'd really hate to lose your aerobics class, Anna."

"I'll bet Mr. Clark would let you stay," Elizabeth said to Anna. "Did you see his face after you answered Mr. Bowman's question? He was grinning from ear to ear!"

"Right before he left, I heard him tell Mr. Bowman to keep up the good work," Jessica added.

Cammi smiled shyly. "I'm in all of your classes, Anna," she said. "It would be easy for me to translate."

Instead of answering out loud, Anna signed back. "You don't have to do this," she replied. "I know it might be hard on you."

Cammi smiled ruefully. "People already think I'm kind of a nerd," she signed. "So, if you

124

don't mind hanging out with a nerd, I don't mind hanging out with a deaf person!"

"Oh, great," Lila complained. "Now you two are talking a secret language."

"No fair," Belinda added. "Not unless you're going to teach us."

"Think about it," Jessica said. "We wouldn't have to get caught sending notes in class anymore. We could just sign across the room when the teacher wasn't looking."

"Plus," Elizabeth said, "you could talk in the library."

"I already talk in the library," Jessica said.

"I know. But if you spoke ASL, you could do it without driving *me* crazy when I'm trying to read."

Anna grinned at Cammi and made a single, quick sign. Cammi smiled back and made the same sign.

"OK, so what did that mean?" Elizabeth asked.

Anna repeated the gesture, intertwining her two index fingers and then reversing them. "That's the sign for *friend*."

Elizabeth mimicked the gesture a little clumsily, first to Anna, and then to Cammi. "Friends," she said out loud. "Hey, I need another one. What's the sign for *Cammi, your profile for the next Sixers is due*?"

"I don't think you're ready for a message that

complicated," Cammi said with a grin. "But I promise I'll get on that rewrite right away."

"Great, but there's one major change. This time it's going to be a double profile," Elizabeth said, "of the two of you."

"We'll call it 'The Dynamic Duo,' " Amy said with a laugh.

"Come on, Anna," Cammi said. "Let's go talk to Mr. Clark. I want him to meet your new ears."

"Look, he's actually smiling," Jessica remarked that afternoon, shaking her head regretfully. "In a few hours he'll be pounded into the dirt, and he's still smiling."

Lila gazed over at Jake, who was cheerfully rummaging through his locker. "It's only because he doesn't *know* he's going to be pounded into the dirt," she said. "If he knew, he'd be crawling inside that locker and locking the door."

"Well, aren't you two going to warn him?" Mandy demanded. By now, most of the Unicorns knew all about Cathy and Jake—thanks to Ellen. "Steven is a lot bigger than Jake," Mandy added. "He'll squash him like a bug."

"Like a bug," Lila repeated with obvious satisfaction.

"Just because you're mad at him, there's no reason not to try to stop this fight," Mandy chided. "Besides, I'll bet Jake would really be grateful if someone warned him."

Lila cast her a sidelong glance. "You know, you may be right, Mandy," she said slowly. "Jake would realize right away who really cared about him."

"Hey, you're talking about the sleazebag who stole my brother's girlfriend," Jessica protested. Still, she was kind of relieved at the idea of Lila breaking up the fight. She didn't want Steven getting into any kind of serious trouble. And he *had* looked awfully furious. There was no telling what he was capable of doing to poor Jake.

"Jessica," Lila said patiently, "don't you know that violence never solves anything?" She turned on her heel and headed toward Jake with Jessica and Mandy following close behind.

"Hi, Lila," Jake said.

"I know something that may interest you," Lila said.

"What's that?"

"You may be in real trouble. Big trouble."

"Oh?" Jake said, looking at Lila doubtfully. "What kind of trouble?"

"It's not a *what*, it's a *who*," Lila said.

"Steven's going to beat you up for stealing Cathy," Jessica blurted.

Lila spun around, eyes blazing. "I was going to tell him!" she cried.

"Steven's going to beat me up, huh?" Jake said, squaring his shoulders. "Fine. I'm not afraid to fight for the girl I love."

Jessica's jaw dropped. "You're not?"

"The girl you *love*?" Lila demanded.

"Yes, the girl I love," Jake said, gritting his teeth. "And if Steven wants to fight me for her— well, let him try!"

Without another word, he slammed the door of his locker and stalked away.

"Nice job, Lila," Mandy said. "You really patched that up. Maybe you should get a job at the United Nations."

When the last-period bell rang, Jessica sprinted from the room. She hoped she could get to Steven and Jake in time to stop the fight. But if that wasn't possible, then at least she didn't want to miss it.

Unfortunately, word of the fight had spread through the school like wildfire, and everyone had the same idea. The hall was packed with people jostling to get outside.

"Jessica!" a voice called as Jessica shoved her way to the front entrance.

To her shock, there, just beyond the lobby door, stood Cathy. Jessica's first impulse was to try to disappear, but there was no way to escape with the crowd surging around her.

"Jessica, you have to listen to me," Cathy wailed as she pulled Jessica aside.

"What do *you* want, you—you traitor?" Jessica demanded.

"Listen to me, Jessica," Cathy said in a pitiful

voice. "I tried to warn Steven, but he wouldn't listen to me."

"Tried to warn Steven? About what?"

"About Jake Hamilton. I know Steven's bigger, but there's something he doesn't realize. Jake has a black belt!"

"Who cares what he's wearing—"

"He's a black belt in karate, Jessica. He's been studying it since he was five years old," Cathy cried. "Don't you see? Steven doesn't have a chance! Jake will destroy him!"

Jessica felt fear clutch at her heart. Was it possible? Jake didn't *look* like any of the guys she'd seen in those old kung-fu movies.

"What's going on?" Lila asked, coming over to them. Suddenly she recognized Cathy. "Oh," she said with a sneer. "It's you. The other woman."

"Never mind that, Lila," Jessica said frantically. "Cathy says Jake is a karate expert!"

"He never told me that."

"He can kill with his bare hands," Jessica cried.

Lila looked thoughtful for a moment. "Well, that's no fun. I was planning to rush to his side when he was lying crushed in the dirt. Then I was going to nurse him back to health."

"We have to stop the fight!" Jessica wailed. She tore away from Cathy's grip and raced across the grass. It was easy to see where the fight was being held. A huge circle of kids were gathered around, cheering and yelling.

"Let me through, let me through!" Jessica cried, pushing her way through the crowd until she burst into an open space.

There were Steven and Jake, only a few feet apart. They were each crouched low, their faces menacing.

"No!" Jessica screamed. She leapt between them, holding her arms out wide to separate the two boys. "Stop this fight!"

"Why?" Steven asked.

The crowd fell silent. All eyes were glued to Jessica. "Because," she began hesitantly, "because it's uncivilized, that's why."

She waited for a moment. Steven and Jake both stood motionless. As long as she kept talking, Jessica felt sure the fight wouldn't start.

"People should learn to get along together, to settle their differences peacefully," she continued. "After all, we're not animals."

Jessica could feel the emotion welling up in her. This was really a pretty great speech she was giving. It only proved that she was going to be an incredible actress someday. "Please," she begged, "can't we all just sit down together? We could talk about this man to man—I mean, man to man to woman—over a milk shake at Casey's."

"A milk shake at Casey's?" Steven echoed.

"Who would pay?" Jake demanded.

Jessica's heart leapt. They were actually listening to her! "I'll pay," she volunteered. "If it means peace."

Steven shrugged good-naturedly. "OK," he agreed. "Sounds good."

Jessica stared at her brother in disbelief. Had she really been *that* convincing? He seemed to be taking this awfully well.

"How about you, Jake?" Steven asked. "You want to let Jessica buy us a shake?"

"Sure," Jake replied. "Only I'd like some fries, too."

"Maybe a burger," Steven added thoughtfully.

Suddenly Cathy entered the circle and joined them, putting her arm around Steven's waist. "Personally, I'd like a banana split," she said. "All this acting makes me hungry."

Jessica watched in stunned silence as Cathy gave Steven a kiss. When Cathy stepped back, she was grinning. So was Steven. So was Jake.

"Acting?" Jessica managed to choke out.

"Steven called me yesterday," Jake explained as the whole group walked to Casey's. "He told me he wanted me to play along with a trick on you, Jessica."

"Yeah, I told him I needed to teach you a lesson about being nosy," Steven said. "See, I knew right away that Cathy wasn't going out with Jake behind my back."

"But I thought—" Jessica began.

"I know what you thought, Jessica," Cathy said. "But you were wrong. That wasn't *Jake* and me in the rocks, it was *Steven* and me. Jake had just been walking toward the rocks with me."

"I headed on down the beach," Jake said. "Actually, I was looking for Lila. I thought maybe she'd gone for a walk."

Around her, Jessica heard the annoying sound of laughter—at her expense. "But I was so sure," she murmured.

"You were wrong," Steven said flatly. "I always knew I could trust Cathy."

Jessica looked over at Elizabeth for support.

"I hate to say I told you so," Elizabeth said, shaking her head. "But let's face it. I did."

"Jessica, how could you *ever* have accused Jake of this?" Lila demanded, walking close to Jake's side. "I'm ashamed of you."

Jessica threw up her hands. "OK, OK. You win. All of you. I'll never stick my nose into your business again. *Now* are you satisfied?"

"No," Jake said.

"Definitely not," Cathy agreed.

"First, we're going to spend all of your savings at Casey's," Steven said. "*Then* we'll be satisfied."

Twelve

◇

"Will you have parties every weekend?" Cara asked Cammi. It was two weeks later, and Cammi and her sister were busily setting food out on the dining-room table.

"Hey, give me a chance," Cammi whispered as she opened a bag of potato chips. She peeked out into the living room, where eight girls were watching Anna open birthday presents. "This *is* my first party, you know," she told Cara. "And Anna doesn't have a birthday every weekend."

"No," Cara said as she reached for a potato chip. "But *somebody* does!"

"How's it going?" Mrs. Adams asked, walking into the room with Mr. Adams.

"So far, so good," Cammi signed. She still couldn't believe it. Elizabeth, Amy, Julie—there were so many people in her very own house. Even Jessica had come.

"Ready for the cake?" Mrs. Adams asked.

Cammi nodded.

"I'll turn off the lights," Cara said, dashing into the living room.

Together, Cammi and her parents carried the cake out, candles flaming. Anna looked up in surprise as they placed it in front of her on the coffee table. "It's beautiful," she signed to Mrs. Adams.

As the group began to sing "Happy Birthday," Cammi, Cara, and Mr. and Mrs. Adams signed the words to the song. Cammi looked over at her parents and felt something strange and very wonderful—something she'd never let herself feel before. She felt proud.

After the cake had been eaten and the last present unwrapped, Anna pulled Cammi into the hallway.

"Here," Anna said. She reached into her back pocket and pulled out a tiny box wrapped in shiny gold paper.

"But it's *your* birthday," Cammi exclaimed.

"Go ahead," Anna urged. "Open it."

Cammi unwrapped the little box excitedly. She peeled back a layer of tissue to reveal a silver necklace. On it was a round silver disk.

"I had it made especially for you," Anna said.

"It's beautiful," Cammi whispered as tears came to her eyes.

"Read the other side," Anna said.

Cammi turned over the silver disk and there, engraved on its surface, was a picture of two index fingers intertwining.

"What do you call that phone thingie again?" Jessica asked as she settled into her sleeping bag in Cammi's room.

"A TDD," Cammi answered.

"Boy, I'd give anything to have one of those around my house," Jessica said.

"How come?" Cammi asked.

"So Steven wouldn't butt into my phone calls," Jessica said.

"You're the one who's been butting in lately," Elizabeth reminded her.

"I *knew* you were going to say that," Jessica said, rolling her eyes.

"Well, I hope you've learned your lesson," Elizabeth said.

"I knew you were going to say *that*, too," Jessica replied.

"Maybe she can read your mind, Elizabeth," Amy teased. "Be careful what you think."

"Yeah, right," Elizabeth said skeptically. She closed her eyes. "What am I thinking now, Jess?"

"Give me a minute," Jessica replied, squeezing her eyes shut in concentration. Suddenly her eyes flew open. "I am *not* insane, Elizabeth Wakefield!"

Elizabeth opened her eyes and gasped. "How'd you do that?"

"Wow," Anna said. "Maybe there really is something to this."

Can Jessica really read Elizabeth's mind? Find out in Sweet Valley Twins and Friends No 70, PSYCHIC SISTERS.

We hope you enjoyed reading this book. If you would like to receive further information about available titles in the Bantam series, just write to the address below, with your name and address: Kim Prior, Bantam Books, 61–63 Uxbridge Road, Ealing, London W5 5SA.

If you live in Australia or New Zealand and would like more information about the series, please write to:

Sally Porter   Kiri Martin
Transworld Publishers   Transworld Publishers (NZ) Ltd
(Australia) Pty Ltd   3 William Pickering Drive
15–25 Helles Avenue   Albany
Moorebank   Auckland
NSW 2170   NEW ZEALAND
AUSTRALIA

All Bantam and Young Adult books are available at your bookshop or newsagent, or can be ordered from the following address: Corgi/Bantam Books, Cash Sales Department, PO Box 11, Falmouth, Cornwall, TR10 9EN.

Please list the title(s) you would like, and send together with a cheque or postal order to cover the cost of the book(s) plus postage and packing charges of £1.00 for one book, £1.50 for two books, and an additional 30p for each subsequent book ordered to a maximum of £3.00 for seven or more books.

(The above applies only to readers in the UK, and BFPO)

Overseas customers (including Eire), please allow £2.00 for postage and packing for the first book, an additional £1.00 for a second book, and 50p for each subsequent title ordered.

Don't miss the extra-long special editions of this top-selling
teenage series starring identical twins Jessica and Elizabeth
Wakefield and all their friends.

SUPER EDITIONS

THE CLASS TRIP
THE UNICORNS GO HAWAIIAN

SUPERCHILLERS

THE GHOST IN THE GRAVEYARD
THE CARNIVAL GHOST
GHOST IN THE BELL TOWER

SWEET VALLEY HIGH

The top-selling teenage series starring identical twins Jessica and Elizabeth Wakefield and all their friends at Sweet Valley High. One new title every month!